TONY CORREIA

JAMES LORIMER & COMPANY LTD., PUBLISHERS
TORONTO

James Lorimer & Company Ltd., Publishers acknowledges funding support from the Ontario Arts Council (OAC), an agency of the Government of Ontario. We acknowledge the support of the Canada Council for the Arts, which last year invested $153 million to bring the arts to Canadians throughout the country. This project has been made possible in part by the Government of Canada and with the support of Ontario Creates.

Cover design: Tyler Cleroux
Cover image: iStock

Library and Archives Canada Cataloguing in Publication

Correia, Tony, author
        Prom kings / Tony Correia.

(Real love)
Issued in print and electronic formats.
ISBN 978-1-4594-1407-5 (softcover).--ISBN 978-1-4594-1408-2 (EPUB)
        I. Title. II. Series: Real love (Series)

PS8605.O768P76 2019   jC813'.6   C2018-905319-4
                                               C2018-905320-8

Published by:	Distributed in Canada by:	Distributed in the US by:
James Lorimer &	Formac Lorimer Books	Lerner Publisher Services
Company Ltd., Publishers	5502 Atlantic Street	1251 Washington Ave. N.
117 Peter Street, Suite 304	Halifax, NS, Canada	Minneapolis, MN, USA
Toronto, ON, Canada	B3H 1G4	55401
M5V 0M3		www.lernerbooks.com
www.lorimer.ca		

Printed and bound in Canada.
Manufactured by Friesens Corporation in Altona, Manitoba,
Canada in December 2018.
Job # 250168

For Dean Mirau.

01 The Wreck Room

On my last report card, my English teacher wrote, "Charlie is outgoing and a self-starter. But he can be bossy." I thought it was a compliment. But my dad didn't see it that way.

"What's so wrong with being bossy?" I asked at the time. "I get stuff done."

"You need to socialize more with people your age. Outside of sitting on committees at school, that is," Dad had said.

That was how I ended up going to the youth drop-in at outNproud. The name is kind of last week if you ask me. It sounds more like a gay breakfast cereal than a queer community centre in downtown Vancouver. I'm not complaining, though. Dave, our ginger-bear peer counsellor, loves to remind us how lucky we are. We have a place to come to twice a week and hang out with queers our age.

"It's not like when I was your age," Dave says. "I had to sneak into gay bars to meet other people like me." I like Dave a lot, but he can sound like a parent trying to get their kid to eat their veggies.

I used to think outNproud was where depressed LGBTQ teens went to discuss their feelings. My friend Geeda told me what it really was like. Geeda and I met at our school's gay-straight alliance. Unlike me, Geeda has no problem socializing. Geeda is Asian and is always trying new stuff with her hair and clothes. People flock to her at school. She's also bi, which means she can have just about anyone she wants at school.

The youth drop-in is nicknamed the Wreck Room,

after Wreck Beach, the nude beach near the University of British Columbia campus. It's decorated with IKEA couches and wood shelves with board games and books. In one corner there's an old clothing rack crammed with clothes that are free for the taking. Once I found a polo shirt with the price tags still on it. They also offer also a bra and binder exchange for trans kids.

My favourite part of outNproud is *RuPaul's Drag Race*! I hate most reality shows, but I can't get enough of that show. Dave has a subscription to gay Netflix. The crowd at outNproud varies depending on the night. But a core group of five of us has been working our way through all the seasons of *Drag Race*. We meet every Friday night. Watching *Drag Race* with Geeda, Lottie, Luis, and Chad is what it must be like to go a hockey game. All that cheering and jeering makes me feel like I belong.

We have a strict "no spoilers" rule for anyone who has already seen an episode. We are pretty good about obeying it, except for Chad.

"You kind of remind me of The Vixen, Chuckles,"

Chad says. He's comparing me to one of the season ten queens. "You're both social warriors. And kind of intense."

I hate it when Chad calls me Chuckles. It's his "cute" way of helping people keep our names straight because they both start with C-H-A. As if anyone would mistake me for Chad. We're polar opposites.

Chad is too handsome for his own good. He's got chiselled features and a cleft chin. His body was hot to start with and is made hotter by CrossFit. Chad strikes me as someone who has never been disappointed a day in his life. I would almost find him attractive, except for the stupid man bun on his head.

"I see Charlie as more like Tina Fey," Lottie says.

"Thanks, Lottie," I say.

Lottie is gender-fluid but presents themself as slightly more masculine or boyish. Lottie is short with thick black hair, and a little bit of facial hair on their chin. No matter the weather, Lottie is dressed in a T-shirt, with 501s that have their wallet attached by a chain. They have a deep, raspy voice that sounds like they've been smoking since they were six. But Lottie insists they've never held a cigarette, much less smoked one.

"What do you think, Luis?" Chad asks.

Luis is the quietest person in our little group. He's Mexican and speaks perfect English, but he always seems embarrassed of his accent. I love the way he talks. Everything he says sounds like it should have a guitar strumming in the background.

I admire how Luis dresses. His plaid shirts are always pressed and buttoned all the way up to the collar. His jeans look like they just came out of the wash. His white Adidas runners could light the way in the dark.

"Well…" Luis says, slowly. He's choosing his words carefully. "I agree that The Vixen and Charlie want to change the world. But I think both of them need to learn how to communicate better."

"Told you so, Chuckles," Chad says.

Luis holds up his finger. "I'm not finished. I have never seen Charlie attack someone the way The Vixen attacked Eureka in front of the judges."

"That's what I've been saying!" Lottie says. They point at me with one stubby finger. "Charlie is Tina Fey."

The episode we're watching ends with The Vixen and Monique Heart lip-synching for their lives. I'm cheering for Monique, but you can see she doesn't know the words to the song. Not knowing your words is the kiss of death on *Drag Race*. Sure enough, RuPaul orders Monique to "sashay away."

Dave stands in front of the TV as the show's credits start to roll.

"I have a quick announcement to make," he says. "OutNproud is starting to plan the queer prom in June. We're looking for volunteers to be on the youth advisory committee. Any takers?"

Chad's hand shoots right up. So does Geeda's. Lottie puts their hand up next. Then, ever so slowly, Luis's hand goes up.

"Don't you want to be part of the committee, Charlie?" Dave asks me. "It's not a lot of work. We just want some input on a theme, a song, and a DJ."

I didn't know there was such a thing as a queer

prom until this very moment. The truth is I really want to be on the advisory committee. But Chad just described me as some sort of militant activist. I worry that joining would open me up to more of his attacks.

"I don't know," I say. "I'm already on the GSA at school. And I'm the treasurer for the student council. I'm not sure I have the time."

"You know you want to," Chad teases.

I try not to let my hatred for Chad make me join the committee. But I'm worried that, with Chad on board, the theme of the prom will be Under the Sea.

"Fine! I'll do it," I say, raising my hand.

"I knew you would," says Chad.

It's a good thing I don't have a pair of scissors in my hand. That man bun would be on the floor already. I pull my bullet journal out of my backpack and open it to my monthly log.

"When do we meet?" I ask.

02 Ride Home

The West End of Vancouver is full of one-way streets. It's almost impossible to get anywhere without zigzagging.

I got my driver's licence and a job at London Drugs as soon as I was old enough. Then I begged my dad to buy me a used car so I wouldn't have to take public transit.

"You know I'm a mechanic for BC Transit, right?" he said when I asked him.

"And you know I hate being at the mercy of someone else's schedule," I told him.

I've needed to control as much of my life as I can, ever since my mom took off without saying goodbye. It's why I sit on so many committees at school. If I have to make my way in this world as an invisible minority, then I want to have a say in the rules.

Dad bought me a "very loved" Volkswagen Golf that I've nearly paid off. It's not a bad car. That is, if you don't mind rolling down your windows by hand and listening to music on CDs.

Geeda and I have become besties ever since I started driving her to and from outNproud. We knew each other from the GSA and student council. But thanks to our drives, she's gotten to know me as a person instead of just someone you can depend on.

"You'd think I'd know my way around here by now," I say. I've got turned around again on the West End streets.

"Why don't you cut across that little paved area right there?" Geeda asks. She points with her phone.

"Because it's illegal," I say.

"This is why I don't drive. Too many rules."

"The reason you don't drive is because it would distract you from your phone," I tease.

I finally get the car going in the right direction.

"I couldn't help but notice," I say. "You didn't defend me against Chad tonight."

"What was there to defend? Chad made a comment. Chad is always making comments."

"But you never actually came out and disagreed with him."

"I don't know why you let Chad get to you," says Geeda. "He's not as confident as you think he is."

"So you agree with him?"

"What makes you say that?"

"Because you're deflecting. If I've learned anything from debating you in class, it's that you always deflect when you're spewing BS."

"Would you mind rephrasing that statement please?"

"Do you think I'm intense?"

Geeda pretends to look at something on her phone.

"Geeda, you're the first real friend I've had in a long time," I say. "Do people think I'm hostile toward them? You would tell me, wouldn't you?"

"Since when do you care what people think?"

"Ever since I learned there was such a thing as a queer prom. Do you know how long I've wanted to go to the prom?"

"This is a side of you I've never seen before." Geeda looks up at me from her phone. "I'm not sure if I should be glad or afraid."

"I've never been to a dance before," I tell her.

"They have them every month at school."

"I wouldn't feel safe at one of those. Remember what happened to Thomas Templeton?"

"That was years ago. The jerks who did that were expelled."

"And Thomas transferred to another school because he was afraid it would happen again," I say. "Despite our school's zero-tolerance policy, they can't police everyone every second of the day. Now tell me if I'm intense to be around."

"Why?"

"Because I want to take a date to the prom."

"Who are you and what did you do with Charlie? I know you're gay. But I never really thought of you as being into guys."

"You think I'm not able to love someone?"

"Okay, this is exactly why I dodged the question."

The traffic on Davie Street is stop and go. We finally reach the traffic light at the top of the hill. After fifteen minutes of driving, we are almost back at outNproud, where we started.

"Look, there's Luis." Geeda points to a figure waiting at the bus stop. "Can we give him a ride?"

"Is this your way of changing the subject?"

Geeda nods.

"As long as he doesn't live in New Westminster," I say.

Geeda rolls down her window and shouts, "Hey, Luis, wanna lift?"

"I'm good. I live too far," Luis shouts back.

"How far?" she yells.

"Near Boundary," he yells back.

"That's fine!" I say. "Tell him to get in the car."

"Hurry up! Get in!" Geeda hollers, waving him over.

Luis isn't even completely in the car before I start driving. We are stopped at the next light before he's finally able to sit up in the back seat.

"Sorry about that," I say. "I hate blocking traffic."

"That's fine," Luis says.

"I don't think I've ever seen you at that bus stop before," I say.

"I've seen you," Luis says. Is he implying that I was ignoring him on purpose? I can't tell.

"You should have said something," I tell him. "I could have been giving you a ride home instead of you taking the bus."

"Charlie really hates buses," Geeda says.

"I don't mind the bus," Luis says. "It gives me time to read."

The car behind us leans on their horn. Luis digs around the back seat for the seat belt.

"So, what brought you to outNproud, Luis?" she asks.

"Nobody knows I'm gay," he replies.

"Aren't you out at school?" I ask.

"I go to a Catholic school," he says. He taps me on the shoulder. "What was that book you were writing in? It looked cool."

"That's Charlie's OCD journal," Geeda tells him. "He uses it to manage his life to the last millisecond. I get tense every time he opens it."

"It's not an OCD journal," I say. "It's a bullet journal. I'll show it to you next time at outNproud."

I drop Luis off after Geeda, since he lives the farthest away.

"Thank you for going out of your way to drive me home," he says.

"It's not that far out of my way," I say. "I live in Hastings Sunrise. We're almost neighbours."

"Do your parents know you're gay?" he asks.

"Parent. Singular. I live with my dad. My mom took off before I started high school."

"I'm sorry," Luis says.

"I'm over it," I lie.

I can see the roller coaster at the Pacific National Exhibition off in the distance. Luis guides me toward his part of the city.

"You can let me off here," he says. He points at a corner. "I don't want my parents to see me get out of your car. The fewer lies I have to tell, the better."

Luis gets out of the car and waves goodbye. I wait until he disappears into the dark before I drive away. On my way home, I feel kind of bad that I've never noticed Luis at the bus stop before. Am I so busy trying to control my life that I'm not seeing what's happening in front of my face?

03 New Kid on the Block

Geeda and I have learned that you have to get to outNproud early on Friday nights. It's the only way to get a seat on the couch for *Drag Race*. Once we've claimed our places, we take turns going to the bathroom and getting food from the snack table.

I notice a new face enter the Wreck Room. He's tall and his skin is the colour of dark wood. His hair is short on the sides. The tight curls on top look sun-bleached. A scarf is draped loosely around his neck, and his clothes look like they came from a boutique. I try not to stare. But then Geeda asks me, "Who is that guy?"

"I don't know. But he's cute," I observe.

"He looks like a musician."

"Or an artist."

We watch Dave greet the new guy. They shake hands and smile as they talk to each other. Dave tells him to help himself to the snacks on the table.

"I wouldn't eat those if I were you," I call out to him.

"These?" he asks, pointing at the pastries.

"They usually put the day-olds out first," I explain. "The gourmet donuts and fancy cupcakes come out halfway through *Drag Race*."

"Thanks for the advice," he says. He has a French accent. I'm a sucker for accents. He walks over to where we're sitting. "I'm Andre."

"I'm Charlie," I say. "This is Geeda."

"Nice to meet you," Andre says. "I just moved here from Montreal a few weeks ago."

"That would explain your accent," Geeda says.

"Obviously," Andre says, rolling his eyes. This would annoy me coming from any other person. But when Andre rolls his eyes it's kind of sexy.

"Want to sit with us?" I ask.

Geeda glares at me. But she scoots over when Andre says yes. Luis comes in and scopes the room for a place to sit. He sees us on the couch.

"Looks like I'm sitting on the floor," Luis says.

"Luis, this is Andre," I say. "He's from Montreal."

"Bonjour!" Luis says. "That's all the French I know."

"This is the most English I've spoken in years," Andre says. "Sometimes I have to translate a word in my mind before I say it."

Geeda pretends to throw up behind Andre's back.

"How do you like Vancouver, Andre?" I ask. I try to say his name as French as I can.

"All the buildings look the same and there isn't much in the way of culture," Andre answers. "What do gay people our age do for fun in this city?"

"This," I say.

"I was afraid of that." Andre frowns.

"Vancouver is fun," Geeda says. "You just need to know where to look."

"In the meantime, there is always *Drag Race*," I say.

"Hey, everybody." Lottie calls over when they see us. "Looks like I'm too late for a spot on the couch."

"Sorry, Lottie," Geeda says.

"Lottie, meet Andre," I say.

"Nice to meet you," Lottie says. They look around the room. "Where's Chad?"

"He's probably styling his man bun," I say.

"Don't be mean, Charlie," Luis says.

"Who is Chad and why does he have a man bun?" Andre asks.

"He's a privileged white guy who thinks he knows everything," I say.

"Charlie, you're white," Luis points out.

"And a guy," Lottie adds.

"But I'm not privileged," I say.

"Being white and male is a privilege," Luis says.

"Trust me, I'm Mexican."

"I don't know this Chad," Andre scoffs. "But he can't know much about fashion if he's walking around with a man bun."

I think I'm in love.

"Do you watch *Drag Race* at home?" Geeda asks.

"Ever since I was eight," Andre says. "My mother got me hooked on it. She knew I was gay before I did."

"We're halfway through season ten right now," I say.

"I loved season ten!" Andre says. "I couldn't believe it when —"

"Wait!" the four us say at the same time.

"None of us have seen this season before," I explain.

"Who was your favourite queen, Andre?" Lottie asks.

"The Vixen, by far. She looks like she belongs in *Vogue*. Plus, I like that she presses people's buttons."

Oh my God. Andre and I are perfect for each other.

Dave connects his tablet to the TV and starts streaming the show for us. I barely pay attention to what's on the screen. All I can think about is whether or not Andre likes me as much I like him.

After the show is over, we get up from the couch to mingle.

"I know this is only your first day here, Andre," I say. "But all of us are on the youth advisory committee for the queer prom. I'm sure there's room for one more if you want to join."

"I would love that," Andre says. "I want to be an event planner someday."

"Perfect! I'll tell Dave."

Andre excuses himself to go to the bathroom. I check out his ass as he walks away. Luis punches me in the shoulder. It brings me back to reality.

"Ouch! What was that for?" I say.

"Your eyes were glued to the seat of his pants," Luis says.

"So? I'm still a man! Remember?"

"I can't believe you asked him to join the advisory committee." Luis shakes his head.

"I was just being nice," I say. "Besides, I think he likes me."

"I'm with Luis," says Geeda. "That guy is so full of himself. Did you hear the way he trashed Vancouver? I've been to Montreal. It's not that great."

"Seriously, Geeda?" Lottie says. "Montreal is pretty awesome."

"Okay, I'll admit Montreal is an amazing city," Geeda relents. "But it's freezing there in the winter."

Luis is still frowning. "I wish you had waited until you got to know Andre better before you asked him to join the committee. He strikes me as the type of person who will make it all about him."

"You've known the guy for less than an hour," I say.

"I think you have something in your eyes, Charlie," Lottie says.

"What?" I wipe my eyes with my fingers.

"Stars!" Lottie says. "You have a crush on that guy."

"I'm just being friendly," I say.

"If that's friendly, I would hate to see what love looks like," Lottie says.

"Shh! Here he comes."

Andre would have to be an idiot not to know we were talking about him. But he doesn't seem to mind. In fact, he seems to enjoy it.

The five of us grab Catan from the games shelf and play a game. Luis and Lottie are the only ones who really understand the rules enough to take the game seriously. I sneak glances at Andre every chance I get. I don't know how, but I'm going to get Andre to go to the prom with me.

04 Bullet Journal

I bring my bullet journal to the first meeting of the youth advisory committee for the queer prom. I've been using one for about a year now. People at school think I'm OCD whenever I pull it out to make an entry. I think what drives people nuts about my journal is the effort I put into writing each thing down that I need to do. Geeda says every entry I make takes an hour off of my life. She thinks it's like smoking a cigarette.

They can make fun all they want. The journal helps me get a better look at the big picture that is my life.

"How does your bullet journal work?" Luis asks. We are waiting for the meeting to start when I open my journal on my lap.

"You don't want to know," Geeda says. "It takes being organized to a whole new level."

"It's actually a really simple way of organizing your life once you get the hang of it," I say. I move closer to Luis to show him how my journal is laid out. "As you can you see, it has five sections: the index, daily log, monthly log, rapid log, and future log."

Geeda leans her head back on the couch and pretends to snore.

"Ignore her," I say. "I use the daily log to keep track of what I need to do today. The monthly log tracks what I'm doing in the coming weeks. And the future log is just a normal calendar where I set goals."

"What is the rapid log for?" Luis asks.

"That's how I keep track of my progress," I say.

"These symbols mark what I've started and finished."

"You know they have an app for that," Geeda says.

"This is more personal than an app," Luis says.

"Thanks, Luis," I say. At least someone likes my style.

"Is everyone here?" Dave asks as he enters the Wreck Room.

"We're still waiting for Chad and Andre," Lottie says.

Maybe Chad already got bored with the idea of being on the committee. With any luck he has blown us off. Only people with nothing else to do on a sunny Saturday afternoon would want to be indoors. He's probably hiking the Grouse Grind or paddleboarding at Jericho Beach.

"Let's give them five more minutes," Dave says.

"Sorry I'm late," Andre says as he breezes into the Wreck Room.

Andre is like a breath of fresh air. I feel like a balloon floating to the ceiling on the air currents he creates.

But right behind Andre is Chad. Andre looks back at Chad and smiles. There's a glint in Andre's eyes when he looks at him. I can see him falling for Chad's charms in front of my eyes. I wonder if anyone would notice if I punched myself in the stomach right now.

How is this possible? They only just met on the stairs. And already they look like they've known each other for years. I thought Andre likes prickly people. How could he go from flirting with me to flirting with Chad so quickly?

"Is that a brick in your lap, Chuckles? Or are you just happy to see me?" Chad points to my bullet journal. Andre laughs at Chad's joke, adding insult to injury.

"It's my bullet journal." I try to hide the book with my body. I can't believe how embarrassed I feel. I normally don't care when people tease me. But this is unbearable.

Chad looks like he's going to ask what a bullet journal is. But Geeda stops him. "Don't ask what it is," she says. "You don't want to know."

Whose side is Geeda on?

"Can we get the meeting started?" Dave says. "I love you like my children. But I would like to rollerblade around the Seawall before it gets dark."

Dave stands in front of the whiteboard on one of the walls. On it, he writes, "Themes." He underlines the word for emphasis.

"Who has an idea for a theme?" Dave asks us.

Chad puts up his hand and says, "Under the Sea!"

"I knew you would say that," I hear myself say to him. Why do I have to say every thought that goes through my head?

"I agree with Charlie," Lottie says. "Anything but Under the Sea."

"What's wrong with Under the Sea?" Chad asks.

"It's been done a hundred million times," I say. "Haven't you ever watched a teen movie? The theme of the prom is always Under the Sea."

"There's a reason for that," Dave offers. "It's cheap and easy to do."

"Do you have a better idea, Chuckles?" Chad asks.

"As a matter of fact, I do." I turn to the page in my bullet journal. "I was thinking we could do an eighties theme."

"The eighties have been done to death," Andre says. He just dismissed my idea without even thinking about it! "I don't know what everyone loves about the eighties. They were tacky."

"I was a teenager during the eighties," Dave says. "And I think they're fabulous. Am I writing any of these ideas down?"

"Write them both down," Geeda suggests.

"Does anyone else have any ideas?" asks Dave.

"How about A Night at the Opera?" Andre says. "We can make everyone wear masks and fill the place with candles and bunting."

"That sounds like it would cost a lot," Luis says.

"I'm sure we could find some business to donate decorations," Andre says.

"Let's not get bogged down with cost just yet," Dave says. "Don't be shy, kids. No idea is a bad idea."

"Tell that to Chuckles," Chad says. "He didn't like mine."

"Because it was a bad idea." I sound more forceful than I intend.

"Charlie!" Dave says. "This is a safe space. I won't stand for outbursts like that."

I resist the urge to say that Chad started it. "Sorry," I mumble.

"Don't say sorry to me," Dave says. "Say sorry to Chad."

Dave can't be serious. But he is.

"Sorry, Chad," I say.

"Apology accepted," Chad says. He smirks at Andre. I totally feel like I've been put in my place.

Dad is watching *Friends* on Netflix when I get home from the meeting. I drop my backpack on the floor and plop onto the couch next to him.

"Did you guys come up with a theme?" Dad asks.

"Yes. Glitter Ball," I say. "There's going to be a mirror ball and lots of silver."

"Isn't that every prom ever?"

"Yeah. After listening to about a hundred ideas

for prom themes, I realized that they pretty much all involve shiny things."

"Why don't you do Under the Sea?" Dad asks.

"Not you, too!"

"What's wrong with Under the Sea? It's a classic!"

"When you put it that way it sounds more fun. It sounded tacky when Chad suggested it."

"Who's Chad?"

"Chad is my nemesis at the drop-in. People assume that he's interesting because he's rich and handsome. But he's dumb as a doornail."

"Sounds like you're jealous of his looks," Dad says, sounding like a dad. "Have you even tried to get to know him?"

"He's always picking on me. I can't like him."

"Some people pick on the people they want to like them."

"It's not working. I just wish I didn't have to work as hard to get people to like me as Chad does."

"Have you ever thought that maybe Chad isn't working at it?"

"What's that supposed to mean?"

"Charlie, you're your own kind of weird," Dad says instead of answering. "You need to stop focusing on Chad. You need to figure out a way to make your weird appealing to other people."

I think Dad is trying to give me advice. But I don't know what he's trying to tell me. It's moments like these when I wonder if I wasn't switched at birth.

05 Advice

I'm in science class. I can't stop thinking about Andre. It's making me crazy. I've had crushes on boys before, but nothing like this. It's like watching a teen movie on a loop. I keep seeing us at a diner, sharing a milkshake. I see us walking hand in hand to a pop soundtrack.

"Are we keeping you awake, Charlie?" Mr. Sheridan asks.

"Yes. I mean, no," I say. "I'm mean, sorry. I have a lot on my mind."

"Would you care to share it with the rest of the class?"

"No, thanks."

Mr. Sheridan is such a homophobe. I always need to be on my game with that guy. I can't help noticing how he lets all the deadbeats nod off in class. But the moment I drift off, it's a major crime.

I'm relieved when class is over. As I walk to my next class, I start to notice the couples holding hands in the halls. Most of the couples at school are legacy relationships from grade school. Take Colin Jones and Maria Estevez. They've been dating since kindergarten. Most of the girls at school wish they could be Maria. I don't get it. I'm all for monogamy. But even I have my limits. I mean, it's like they're still the little kids they were when they met.

I've yet to see a same-sex couple holding hands in the halls. Our school has a strict no-bullying policy. If someone attacked you for being gay, they would be expelled. That's great after the fact. But who wants to go through the pain of getting beat up?

The crazy thing is, all the straight kids think the

queers are having all the sex. They don't know how good they have it. I would kill to see more queer kids dating at school so I could see how it's done. You would think the GSA would help in that respect. But all we talk about is creating safe spaces.

I try to think of who I can ask for advice. Then it hits me. Geeda! Geeda goes on dates with both sexes. She'll know what to do.

I find Geeda at lunch sitting with the other pretty girls in our grade. All of them are looking at their phones when I walk up to their table.

"Hey, Geeda," I say. All four of the girls look up from their screens at me. I feel like an artifact in a museum.

"Hey, Charlie!" says Geeda. "What brings you to this side of the cafeteria?"

"Could I could get your help with something?"

"Is everything okay?" she asks. "You have a weird look on your face."

"It's not a serious problem. Just kind of embarrassing."

"Those are my favourite problems."

We leave the cafeteria. We end up out at the bleachers where no one can hear us.

"What's eating you, Charlie?" Geeda asks. "Did they cut the budget for the student council?"

"I have a crush on a boy."

"Not Andre from outNproud?"

"What's wrong with Andre?"

"He's attractive and everything. But he's kind of mean."

"I think you're confusing being mean with having an opinion."

"So what's the problem?"

"He likes Chad."

"Everyone likes Chad. Chad is attractive. Therefore, he is likeable."

"That's the problem. When I met Andre, I got the feeling he likes prickly people like me. But the moment Chad entered the scene I became invisible."

"Why don't you send Andre a dick pic? Isn't that what guys do?"

"I'm being serious."

"So am I. I bet you I have a dick pic of every guy playing on the field on my phone right now." Geeda holds out her phone. "Want to see?"

"I'm not sending anyone a picture of my dick," I say. "With my luck, my dad would find it."

"It hurts me to see you so torn up about this guy." Geeda puts an arm around me. "You never struck me as someone who cared about dating."

"What's that supposed to mean? I want to fall in love as much as the next person!"

"I thought you had more important things on your mind. But I'm glad you're putting yourself out there."

"What am I going to do? I'm in way over my head here. I can't organize my way into someone's heart."

"You could start by acting like you're interested in the guy."

"It's not obvious already?"

"You don't act like someone with a crush when you're around him."

"And here I thought I was making an idiot of myself."

"Give it time. That's bound to happen."

"It was easier being a control freak."

"One thing I know for sure. You're never going to distract Andre from Chad by being a sad sack. Try being a teenager like the rest of us. Enjoy yourself."

"I'm not sure I know I how."

"There's your first problem right there. You know what you need?"

"What?"

"A wingman."

"Like a costume?"

"No! Like a bro. Another gay guy you can confide in and talk about guys with. People are far more attractive when they move in a pack. It's a scientific fact."

"Where am I going to find a wingman? You're my only friend at school."

"Why don't you ask Luis from outNproud? He seems like a nice guy."

"He's kind of quiet, isn't he?"

"Maybe he just needs to get know you better. He seems to have opened up more since we picked him up from the bus stop."

"But he's not even out to his parents."

"Bitch, please. You can't judge a gay person by how out they are."

She has a point.

"I feel like I'm learning to walk all over again," I whine. "Why couldn't I be born as good-looking and charming as Chad?"

"The world is full of Chads," Geeda says. "If anything, it could use more Charlies."

"Thanks."

"Are you forgetting what RuPaul always says?"

"If you can't love yourself, how in the hell are you going to love somebody else?" we both say at the same time.

The bell rings. I'm starting to feel a little better. Now I just have to get hold of Luis.

06 Wingman

I search for Luis's Facebook profile and send him a direct message as soon as I get home from school.

Want to hang out sometime? I write. Luis responds almost right away. He says he would love to and includes his phone number. I call him as soon I see the message.

"Luis?" I say.

"Charlie?" Luis sounds nervous. Then he lowers his voice and says, "Can I call you right back?"

"Sure."

The phone rings less than three minutes later.

"Sorry about that," Luis says. "I was afraid my parents would suspect something."

"Because you answered the phone? Straight people talk on the phone all the time."

"My mother was in the room," he explains. "I just wanted to speak freely."

"Where are you now?"

"In the parking garage." I can hear his voice echo, bouncing off the cement. He still lowers his voice when he speaks, even though he's not at home. I feel bad for him. My dad wasn't exactly thrilled when I came out to him. But he wasn't surprised, either. I can't imagine what it would it be like having to live a double life. Especially at home.

Well, here goes. "I was thinking about doing a teen movie double feature this weekend," I say. "Want to join me? I can drive you to and from home, if you like."

"I would love to come," Luis says.

"Will it be okay with your parents?"

"I'll lie. I'll say I'm going to a friend's place to study."

"Won't they suspect anything?"

"My parents don't know my Canadian friends. I can do almost anything I want as long it involves studying. I tell them I'm at Spanish Club when I go to outNproud. But I can't stay out late."

"I promise to have you home by ten p.m."

"That would be perfect."

Luis and I set up a time to meet on Saturday. As soon as I get off the phone, I wonder if Luis thinks I was asking him out on a date.

Luis takes the bus to my place. I meet him at the Dairy Queen that closed down. That way he wouldn't get lost trying to find our building.

"I've gone by this area so many times on the bus," Luis says. "I always wondered what it was like."

"It has definitely improved since the hipsters found it," I say. "Growing up, I avoided Hastings Street after dark. Now it's the cool part of town."

Dad and I live in a three-storey walk-up that was built in the seventies. Dad moved into the place in the nineties and pays almost nothing in rent — at least by Vancouver standards. We keep waiting for the day when we get evicted and have to leave the city.

"Nice place," Luis says as he enters our apartment.

"Luis, this is my dad," I say, gesturing awkwardly to my father.

"Hello." Luis waves at my dad.

Dad sits up like he's been caught napping on the job. I notice he's acting a little weird. It's like he's being macho and insecure at the same time.

"Hi, Luis," Dad says. "Welcome to our home."

"Dad was just going to watch TV in his room. Weren't you, Dad?" I say.

"Right," Dad says. "If you need me I'll be in my room."

I wait until the door closes behind him.

"Sorry about that," I say to Luis. "Dad's not used to me having friends."

We settle in on the couch. Neither of us has seen *Sixteen Candles* before, so we watch that first.

"Well, that was kind of racist. And a little rapey," I say after the movie is over.

"You forgot homophobic."

"I think we should wash that out of our minds with some *Mean Girls*. What do you think?"

"I think I need a bathroom break," Luis says.

Dad comes out of his room the moment Luis closes the bathroom door.

"Is everything okay?" Dad asks quietly. "You know I don't mind if you kiss, right? But please don't have sex."

"What is wrong with you?" I whisper. How embarrassing! "We're just watching a movie."

The toilet flushes. Dad nearly crashes into Luis on his way back to his room.

I'm never bringing anyone over to our house again.

Luis and I take a break halfway through *Mean Girls* to make popcorn.

"So, do you have a crush on anyone?" I ask Luis.

"What makes you say that?" He starts blushing.

"You're a gay teenage boy. You have to have a crush on somebody."

"I haven't had a crush on a boy since I was in grade seven," he says. "We had just moved to Canada. My English wasn't very good. His name was Jordan. He looked like a movie star."

"Was he gay?"

"I don't know. He was really nice to me at school. So many of the other students weren't."

"What happened?"

"We made plans to go to the movies together. He told me he would meet me at the theatre. But he never showed up."

I'm sorry I asked.

"To be honest, I almost said no when you invited me to your house," Luis says.

"So what made you decide to say yes?"

"I'm tired of hiding from the world."

"Do you want to know who I have a crush on?"

"Who?"

"Andre."

"From outNproud?" Luis sounds surprised. "Gross!"

"What's wrong with Andre?"

"What is the word in English?" Luis crinkles his brow. "He's phony!"

"Geeda doesn't like him, either. Do you think I'm crazy for liking him?"

"Yes! A hundred times, yes. He's a stuck-up jerk!"

"I think that's why I'm attracted to him," I confess. "It doesn't matter. He's obviously in love with Chad."

"That doesn't mean you shouldn't try to date him," Luis says. "Has *Sixteen Candles* or *Mean Girls* taught you nothing? Maybe he just needs the right person to help him see the error of his ways."

"You might be on to something. Maybe the answers to all of my dating problems can be found in teen rom-coms."

"That's not what I meant," Luis says, backtracking.

"Oh, I know the difference between a movie and real life," I say. "But I've never dated before. These movies are the closest thing to a textbook that I have. Do you think your parents would let you stay at my place long enough to watch *Clueless*?"

"I think I can arrange that," Luis says.

Geeda was right. It's fun to have a wingman to do things with. I just wish I had bought more snacks.

07 *Fighting Words*

The next meeting of the youth advisory committee is in full swing. Today we're trying to come up with a prom song. The six of us have spent the last fifteen minutes shouting names of songs at Dave. He is trying to keep up with us, writing the titles on the whiteboard.

"One at a time! One at a time," Dave says, trying to calm us down.

"How about 'Teenage Dream'?" Andre suggests. "It's the perfect prom song."

"I love that song," I say.

"So do I," says Chad. It's like he's trying to outdo me.

"It's too gender-specific," Lottie says.

"I'm with Lottie," Geeda says. "It's kind of a hetero song for a queer prom."

"Then why not 'Born this Way'?" asks Chad.

"If you're going to go with 'Born this Way,' you might as well use 'Express Yourself.' That's the song she stole from Madonna," says Dave. He is using his gay-man-of-a-certain-age voice.

"What does that mean?" Andre asks.

"People think Lady Gaga based 'Born this Way' on 'Express Yourself,'" Geeda says.

"Gaga did write 'Born this Way' in ten minutes," adds Luis.

"It shows," Dave says.

"I've never really embraced that song as a queer anthem," Geeda says.

"Neither have I," Lottie says.

"How about 'Can't Stop the Feeling'?" Geeda suggests.

"Justin Timberlake is so overrated," Andre says.

"I happen to like Justin Timberlake," Geeda says. She looks to Lottie for support. Lottie just shrugs their shoulders. Even Lottie can't get behind Justin Timberlake. "I'm obviously the only cisgender woman in the room."

"You don't have to limit yourself to recent hits, you know," Dave reminds us. "The song you choose should be timeless. You want a song that will remind you of the prom for the rest of your life."

"But we want a song that everyone will know," Andre says.

"How about 'Closer' by Tegan and Sara," Chad suggests.

"That's so old," says Geeda.

"By a couple of years," Lottie points out.

"I love that song," Andre says. He gazes at Chad and says, "It's very romantic. Perfect to dance to with your honey."

I can feel the breeze Andre's lashes make as he bats them at Chad. A wave of jealousy courses through my body. I thought I would have more time to get Andre to notice me. I've barely had time to study the movies Luis and I watched on the weekend. I can already see myself going to the prom alone.

"But is the song a classic?" I ask, trying to break the moment between Andre and Chad.

"I agree with Charlie," Luis says. "It's a fun song to dance to when you want to meet someone. But I don't think it's the right song when you are on a date."

"Chuckles doesn't like it because he can't dance," Chad says.

"There's no need to get personal, Chad," Dave says. "This is a safe space."

"I could dance to that song in my sleep," I say. "I just don't think it's the right song for a Glitter Ball."

"You don't like it because I suggested it, Chuckles," says Chad.

"You two, that's enough," Dave says. "It's just a song."

But it isn't just a song. It was my chance to impress Andre with my taste in music. I haven't even had a chance to come up with a song I can suggest.

"Stop calling me Chuckles," I say. "I'm not a freaking clown."

"You're right," Chad says. "How could anyone confuse you with someone who makes people laugh?"

"Chad, Charlie, can I speak to you two in the hall?" Dave says.

I can't look at the others as I get up and follow Dave out the door. The three of us walk far enough away from the Wreck Room that the others won't hear us.

"What has gotten into the two of you?" Dave says.

"Ask Charlie," says Chad. "He's the one who jumped down my throat."

"That's the first time you've called me by my real name in months," I say.

"That's the first time you've called me by my real name in months," Chad mocks. He does a perfect imitation of me. He must have been practicing for weeks.

My face goes hot. I would pull his hair by the man bun if I didn't think it would get me kicked out of outNproud. I imagine him doing his impression of me for Andre behind my back. I'm dying at the thought of Andre laughing at me.

"I like you both a lot," Dave says. "But if you two behave like that again, I'm kicking you off the committee. Now apologize to each other and learn to get along. There's enough hate to go around without us hating each other."

Chad and I say we're sorry and go back to the Wreck Room. I avoid eye contact with Andre as I take my seat on the couch.

"I think we found our song," Geeda says.

Thank God. I just want to go home.

"What do you guys think of this," Lottie says. Lottie presses play on their phone. It's fast and slow at the same time. I know I've heard it before, but I don't know where.

"That's cool. What is it?" Chad asks.

"'I Melt with You' by Modern English," Dave says, smiling. It's from his era. "It's a perfect prom song."

We listen to it a few more times. I imagine myself dancing with someone beneath a mirror ball. But I can't see their face. It's in the shadow of the light of the mirror ball.

"It's perfect," I say.

"I agree," Chad says. "Good choice, Lottie."

"Don't compliment Lottie," Geeda says. "Luis was the one who found it on Spotify."

I smile. Leave it to my wingman to put an end to this nightmare for me.

Dad is watching *Friends* on Netflix again. I don't know what he sees in that stupid show. I say a quick hello and rush past him to my room. I drop my backpack on the floor and fall flat on my face on my bed.

Dad gently knocks on the door. Then he pokes his head in my room.

"You okay, sport?" he asks.

"Just a little tired between school, work, and all the committees I'm on," I say.

"Let me know if you need anything."

I wait until I hear *Friends* come back on the TV. Then I bury my face in my pillow and start to cry.

08 Spreadsheet

It's been three days since the last committee meeting. I'm still licking my wounds. I'm at my part-time job in the electronics department at London Drugs. I should be on the floor helping customers but I'm too depressed. I've spent most of my shift leaning against the glass display case. I replay Chad's imitation of me over and over in my head.

My phone vibrates in my pocket. It's Luis. It's not like him to call me out of the blue. He usually texts first. We're not supposed to talk on the phone during our shifts. But I don't care.

"Hey, Luis. What's up?" I say quietly.

"I saw how upset you were on Saturday. So I made you a present to make you feel better."

"I wasn't upset." I am lying through my teeth.

"So you were honking at every car on the drive home from the meeting because you were happy?"

"I hate the traffic in this town."

"All right. Just forget about it, then."

"Now I'm curious. What is this present?"

"If you come to my place tomorrow, I can show it to you."

"Will your parents be cool with that?"

"It will just be Mom. My father works nights. I'll tell her you're a classmate. You can't be gay around her, though."

"You mean it isn't written across my forehead?"

"Never mind," Luis says. "If you're going to be like that, I can show you another time."

"I'm sorry, Luis." I can hear the hurt in his voice.

"I shouldn't take my feelings out on you. I would love to come over."

"Can you pick me up from school? It will look better for my mother."

Does he want me to wear a school uniform as well? I'm a little annoyed, but I blow it off. I have to respect his coming-out process.

"Sure. Text me when you get out of class."

The Catholic school kids are trickling out by the time I pick up Luis. He is leaning against a signpost, reading a book on an e-reader. He doesn't see my car approach. I've never noticed how attractive Luis is until now. I'm surprised by how much pleasure I get from seeing him standing there, waiting for me.

I give the horn a gentle tap to let him know I'm here. His face lights up when he sees me. I almost want to give him a peck on the cheek when he gets into the car.

Luis's apartment smells like onions, garlic, and cooked beef. A telenovela blares from the TV. There's a statue of the Virgin Mary on top of the TV and a framed image of The Last Supper above the couch. One wall is full of family photos, including one of Luis at his first communion. He looks adorable with his little white suit and toothy grin.

"Mama, this is Charlie," Luis calls to the kitchen. A woman in her late thirties ducks her head below a row of cupboards. She smiles at me.

"Hello!" she says. "Are you hungry? We have plenty of food."

"No, thank you. I have dinner waiting for me," I say. I'm actually starving. But I'm afraid if I spend too much time around Luis's mom she's going to figure out I'm gay.

"My room is down here," Luis says.

"Keep the door open," Luis's mother calls from the kitchen.

Luis rolls his eyes. "Sorry about that," he says when we're alone.

"I'm not offended."

"I am."

I'm floored by how neat Luis's room is. I thought I was tidy but Luis's room is the bullet journal of bedrooms. The bed looks like it was made by a soldier. There is hardly anything on top of the dresser or the shelves.

"You never told me you were this organized, Luis," I say. "Don't you keep anything personal where you can see it?"

Luis opens a desk drawer. He reaches inside and pulls out a Tony Stark action figure.

"Do you keep him in there because of your mom?" I ask as quietly as I can.

"You don't have to whisper as long as the TV is on," Luis says. "I keep it in there because I don't like clutter."

Luis sits on a stability ball and offers me a small chair. There are two large monitors on top of Luis's desk. There is a wireless mouse and a keyboard that has more keys than I would know what to do with. Luis logs into his computer. A big blob of code appears on the screen as soon as it wakes up.

"I think you could do better than Andre," Luis says. "But I decided to help you go on a date with him before Dave kicks you out of outNproud."

"Thank you for your concern," I say. "But I think that ship has sailed."

"Don't sell yourself short, Charlie. If Andre and Chad aren't dating already, that means there's still time for you to make your move."

"So what do you have in mind?"

"I created a program that looks at all the plots of teen movies from 1990 to today. It will give us some ideas on how to get Andre to notice you."

"You wrote a computer program for me?"

"It's a simple program. All I did was access TMDb with an API."

"Don't you mean IMDb?"

"IMDb doesn't have a public API."

"What's an API?"

"It doesn't matter. What matters is I recorded all the

plot points from the movies. Then I ran a simple loop to check which plots appeared more than once. Then I had the program rank the plot points from highest to lowest."

"Can you say that again in English?"

"Never mind. It's not as complicated as it sounds. Will you do the honours?"

Luis pushes the keyboard toward me. I press the Enter key. The screen comes to life as it scrolls through all sorts of text. It takes about five minutes for the program to compile the data. I hold my breath with anticipation.

The computer spits out the results in broken English:

- Get makeover
- Spill drink on rival
- Good dancer
- Make passionate speech

The last item on the list almost reads like a fortune in a cookie:

- All of your secrets are exposed

"What do you think that means?" I ask, pointing at the screen.

"That only happens to the villain."

"But what if I'm the villain?"

"You're not the villain."

"This list doesn't make any sense," I say. "I can't spill a drink on Chad. I'll get kicked out of outNproud."

"You're missing the most important item on the list," Luis says. "The makeover."

If there's a makeover to be had, we need to get Geeda in on it.

09 *Makeover*

Geeda's eyes well up with tears when I ask if she would give me a makeover. She is so moved, you would think she had won an award.

"It will be an honour and privilege to make you over," Geeda says. "How much time do we have?"

"Can we do it before street outreach?"

Dave asked the advisory committee if we would help out with the outNproud booth at Jim Deva Plaza. It's to build awareness for the drop-in. All of us said yes.

"But that's two days from now!" says Geeda.

"I can't face Chad and Andre as the same old me," I say. "I need a new start."

"Fine, but we're going to need to cut last period tomorrow. There's no other way to get it all done in one evening."

I've never cut class before. I run through the next day's schedule in my mind. My last class of the day is English. I have an A+ in English. I can afford to skip one class if it means looking like a million bucks for Andre.

"I'm in!" I say. "I'll let Luis know when we're coming for him."

We're on our way to pick up Luis from school. Geeda holds up her tablet to show me a dream board of possible looks.

"Notice how I kept things simple," she says. She holds the board in my line of vision. I can just see around it to drive. "I'm thinking a plain white T-shirt. But we'll dress it up with a jaunty vest. And for the pants we have a nice pair of 501 jeans or slim-fit Khakis. Then we'll garnish it with a pair of Converse sneakers."

"I like it," I say. "How much is all this going to cost?"

"Including the haircut? About two hundred dollars."

"I don't have two hundred dollars to spend on clothes!"

"I was just testing the waters," Geeda says. "I'll try to keep it to around a hundred."

Luis barely waits for the car to stop before hopping into the back seat. "Where are we going first?" he asks.

"Jefferson's Barbershop on Commercial Drive," Geeda says. "Get the lead out. Or we'll be late for our appointment."

The barbershop is decorated with old *Star Wars* toys from the seventies and eighties. My dad would go nuts in this place.

The barber drapes a cape across my chest. "What'll it be?"

I look at Geeda in a panic. I normally just get a trim.

"Can you cut it short on the sides and keep it full on top? Like James Dean?" Geeda says.

"Totally!" the barber says.

Twenty minutes later, the barber holds a mirror behind my head. I nod when I see what it looks like from behind and the sides.

"I love it," I say.

"Product for your hair?" he asks.

"Yes!" Geeda says before I have a chance to say no.

When we leave the barbershop, Geeda leads us across the street. A vintage clothing store is having a sale.

"Look at this!" Luis says. He holds up a cool old bowling shirt.

"That's perfect!" Geeda says. "Charlie, try this shirt on with this pair of jeans."

I go into one of the change rooms and slip into the jeans. I can't believe how good they fit. I put the bowling shirt on over my white T-shirt. I step out in my socks for the two of them to see.

"Wait," Geeda says. She gets down on her knees and rolls up the jeans a bit. She stands up and steps back to get a better look at me. "Not bad if I say so myself."

"What do you think, Luis?" I ask.

Luis doesn't say anything at first. I can't tell if he likes it or hates it.

"You look nice, Charlie," he says at last.

"You're not just saying that?" I ask.

"I've never seen you look so attractive before," he says.

I'm flattered by Luis's compliment. He sounds sincere, like he had to work up the nerve to say it. This is a good sign. If I can get Luis's attention in this outfit, I should be able to get Andre to look away from Chad long enough for me to turn on the charm.

Dad is on the couch when I get home. I don't even have to check to see what he is watching.

"How many episodes of that thing are there?" I ask him.

"Thousands," he says. Dad turns away from the TV. He looks surprised to see me. "What happened to you?"

"I got a haircut."

"Are those shopping bags in your hand?"

"Yeah. So?"

"Since when do you buy new clothes before your old ones wear out?"

"A guy needs a fresh look every now and then."

"Does this have something to do with the friend you had over the other week?"

"A little. But not the way you're thinking. Luis is my wingman."

"Your wingman? Are you guys a gay crime-fighting duo?"

"No, he's my friend. He's helping me make a better impression. You're the one who said I need to socialize more."

"So who do you like so much he made you spend money?" Dad asks.

"Come on, Dad. Don't make me talk about that."

"Why not?"

"I don't know. I don't feel comfortable talking about gay stuff with you."

"Do you want to have sex with this guy? This guy who is not your friend Luis?"

"Dad!" I'm turning red. "He barely even knows I'm alive. Why do you think I bought all these clothes and got a haircut?"

"Now this is making more sense. If you ask me, anyone you need to impress isn't worth dating."

"How would you know? You haven't been on a date since mom left."

Dad's face goes white. I meant it as a joke. I had no idea he would take it personally.

"Dad, I'm sorry. I didn't think before I spoke," I say.

"No. You're right. Who am I to give dating advice? I've only been in one relationship. And she left me for someone else."

"Don't you think it's time you got off the couch? Put yourself on the market again?"

"Ugh. I hated going to bars when I was young. I

can't imagine doing it at my age."

"There's always online dating," I suggest.

"That's more depressing than bars," he says.

"Don't knock it until you try it." Then I picture my dad on a dating app. I throw up a little bit in my throat.

"Maybe I should give it a shot," he says. "Who knows? Maybe we could go on a double date some time."

"I don't think the world is ready for that yet."

10 Street Outreach

Geeda, Luis, Lottie, and I are gathering flyers and info sheets about outNproud for the street outreach in Jim Deva Plaza. When Andre walks in the Wreck Room, he looks at me like I'm a stranger. Then it's like everything comes into focus and he realizes it's me.

"Did you cut your hair?" Andre asks.

My knees feel like noodles. "Yeah. I thought it was time for a change."

"And those clothes," he says. "Did three little fairies work their magic on you?"

"Just Geeda," Luis whispers.

"These old things?" I say, trying to get Luis to be quiet. "They were on the floor when I got out of bed!" Geeda told me to say that if Andre noticed my clothes.

"Sorry I'm late," says Chad as he enters the room. "I stopped to get us all some cronuts and coffee." He holds up the box of cronuts and a carton of coffee for us to see.

"Don't you have to order those a year in advance or something?" Lottie asks, awe in their voice.

"My dad knows the owner of the bakery," Chad says.

Of course he does, I think.

"Will someone split a cronut with me?" Geeda says. "I can't eat all those carbs and butter."

"Screw that. I want a whole one," Lottie says. "Two if there's enough to go around."

"I'll split a cronut with you, Geeda," Dave says.

We gorge ourselves on buttery fried dough

and coffee. Next we organize the supplies for the outNproud booth.

Dave hands me his clipboard. "Charlie, would you mind running through my checklist to make sure we have everything? I don't trust myself this early on a Saturday morning."

I take the clipboard in one hand and go to put my cup of orange juice down on a table with the other. Just then, Andre starts to demonstrate The Floss for us. Andre swings his fists behind his back in the first dance move. He hits my hand and knocks my orange juice all over Chad.

Oh my God! It's just like Luis's computer program predicted. I spilled something all over my enemy.

"Gah! I'm so sorry, Chad!" I say.

Chad looks at me like I did it on purpose. But then he sees the look of horror on my face and relaxes. "Don't sweat it, Chuckles," he says. "It was an accident. I can get some clothes from the clothes rack."

The rest of us gather the supplies while Chad picks out some new clothes. He comes back from the bathroom in a cut-off plaid shirt and pair of short denim shorts.

"Are those Daisy Dukes?" Dave asks, pointing to Chad's shorts. "Those were all I wore in the nineties."

"Aren't they great?" Chad says.

"They're amazing," Andre says. His eyes light up, looking at Chad's assets barely covered by the tiny shorts.

We gather the folding table, canopy, and boxes of flyers. Then we head to the plaza. I love Jim Deva Plaza. It was named after the man who opened the first gay bookstore in Vancouver. It's one of the few places to be with other queers that's free and good for all ages.

We set up the booth next to the giant megaphone. Chad connects his phone to a Bluetooth speaker and starts playing some disco tunes. Andre starts to do The Floss. Not to be outdone, Chad starts twerking to the disco beat. Suddenly every guy within a mile of our booth heads toward the table to check them out.

I feel myself becoming invisible. I try to tell

people about the youth drop-in and the queer prom. All their attention is on Chad and his Daisy Dukes. "My eyes are here," I want to say, but it's no use. Information is no match for a good twerk.

"Someone should get them a pole," Lottie whispers.

"Or a thong," I mutter back.

"I need to go to the bathroom," Geeda says. "Want to come with me, Charlie?"

"I'm good," I say.

"I'll go with you, Geeda," says Lottie.

"I wanted to show Charlie something, if that's okay," Geeda explains. She obviously has something to tell me. Lottie looks disappointed.

"Come to think of it, I could use a little break," I say.

Geeda and I cross the street and walk back to outNproud.

"What do you think of Lottie?" Geeda asks me.

"Is that why you dragged me away from the booth? To talk about Lottie's crush on you?"

"Not entirely. But yeah, I wouldn't mind talking about my love life for a change."

"Lottie's great," I say. "But I've never had a crush on a gender-fluid person before."

"Neither have I," Geeda admits.

"At least Lottie is into you. Try competing with Chad and his short shorts."

"About that. Can't you see what's happening between those two?"

"Yeah. Andre and Chad were practically humping each other."

"Then why aren't they a couple?"

"Maybe they're taking it slow."

"No! Chad hasn't sealed the deal!" Geeda punctuates her words by poking me with her finger. "Andre is practically humping Chad's leg. But Chad is afraid to make his move."

"What are you saying?" I ask.

"For all his good looks and charm, I don't think Chad has ever kissed a boy," Geeda says. "Nothing has happened between him and Andre. Because Chad doesn't know what to do next."

It's like a veil has been lifted. Chad isn't a jerk because he's privileged. He's a jerk because he's insecure.

"Does that mean I still have a chance with Andre?"

"A small one. But the door is closing."

"So what do I do now?"

"You need to go in for the kill. Right away, the minute Chad is away from the booth. This could be your only chance."

It's just past noon when I finally get my opening. Dave asks us if anyone is hungry. He volunteers to get us some pizza. "Does someone mind giving me a hand?"

"I'll go," Chad says. "Want to join us, Andre?"

"No. But I think I'll take a break from dancing," he says. Chad looks surprised, like he assumed Andre would follow him anywhere he went. I see Chad look back over his shoulder as he walks away with Dave.

Geeda gestures with her head in Andre's direction, as if to say, "What are you waiting for?"

I get up from the folding chair and walk to the back of the tent. Andre is sitting there, fanning himself.

"I need a break from talking to people," I say to Andre. He looks frustrated. I feel like I'm annoying him. Time for a different tactic. "You're really good at The Floss."

Andre's eyes light up. When in doubt, pay him a compliment.

"Thank you!" he says. "I've been practicing all week. It's not as hard as it looks."

"Would you mind showing me? I've always wanted to learn."

"I would love to."

Andre spends the next ten minutes showing me how to coordinate my hand movements with my hips. People stop to watch us. Some of them get in line to learn how to do The Floss as well.

When Dave and Chad come back with pizza, about ten of us are Flossing together. A crowd has formed around the outNproud booth to watch us. There's a small round of applause when we're finished.

"That was fun," I say. "You're a good teacher, Andre."

"A teacher is only as good as his student," Andre says. He puts his hand on my shoulder. "We should hang out more."

"I'd like that," I say.

"I want to learn how to Floss, too," Chad says.

"Maybe later," says Andre. "Right now I'm starving." He beelines toward one of the boxes of pizza.

Geeda gets my attention. She gives me two enthusiastic thumbs up.

11 Grand Gesture

In science, we're doing review exercises for our final exams. I'm okay at science, but I have to put in the work.

Fifteen minutes into class, the door opens. I panic. What if there's an active shooter in the building? It turns out to be almost as weird. Seven kids walk into the room carrying poster boards. They stand at the front of the class. One by one, they flip the cards over for all of us to see:

Susan,

will

you

be

my

prom

date?

Once the cards are flipped over, Aiden Jenson bursts through the door with a bouquet of flowers. In front of the entire class he says, "Susan Barclay, will you go to the prom with me?"

The next thing I know, Susan is crying and saying yes. The other students are applauding, even our teacher.

WTF? I'm trying to study here!

The whole episode annoys me for about an hour. Who the hell do these straight kids think they are? But the more I think about it, the more I realize they might be onto something. I call Luis at lunch to tell him what happened.

"That's a promposal," he says. "There's been a lot of them at my school lately. It's a lot of work to ask someone on a date, if you ask me."

"I agree. But after the dance routine Andre and I did on the weekend, it might be what I need. I think a promposal is a sure-fire way of getting Andre to go to the queer prom with me. Please say you'll help me."

"Wouldn't Geeda be a better person to ask? This sounds like her sort of thing."

"Geeda's busy sorting out her feelings for Lottie," I say. "I need someone with an organized brain like yours. Someone who can help me put a plan in place."

"I don't know. I still think you can do better than Andre."

"Please, Luis? This is the first time I've ever gone after a boy in my life. This could decide my dating future. Don't you want me to have a good dating future?"

"Okay. I'll do it," he says, finally. "But I still think he's a jerk."

I knew he would.

I'm vacuuming the dust bunnies out from under my bed when Dad comes home from work.

"What's with all the cleaning?" he asks.

"Luis is coming over to help me with a project."

"Is this the guy you have a crush on?"

"No, Luis is my wingman. You met him a couple of weeks ago," I explain. "Luis wrote a computer program to help me to get the guy I have a crush on. Now he's going to help me come up with an idea for a promposal."

"There is so much to unpack from that last statement," Dad says. "First of all, what the heck is a promposal?"

"It's this stupid thing straight kids do to ask people to the prom."

"And what's this about your friend creating an app to help you get a date?"

"It's not an app. It was a computer program. Apparently Luis is some sort of tech genius. I didn't even ask him to do it for me. He just did it on his own."

"First off, writing code is a big deal. I took a class in it in my twenties and I nearly lost my mind. Second, if someone writes a computer program for you without asking, then that's the guy you should have a crush on."

"Luis isn't into guys."

"He's straight?"

"He's gay. But he doesn't care about dating."

"Charlie, you need to put that bullet journal of yours to better use. From where I'm standing, you're chasing the wrong guy."

The intercom buzzes. Dad picks up the old phone near the door and lets Luis into the building. He doesn't even ask who it is.

"You realize you may have just let a burglar into the building," I say.

"The only thing worth stealing is the TV." He shrugs.

"Please don't act weird when he gets here."

"Scout's honour." Dad holds up two fingers and puts the other hand to his heart.

I let Luis in and usher him into my room before

Dad has a chance to break his promise. I pray that Luis can't smell the Febreeze I sprayed all around my room. I remade the bed so that it looks perfect. I hope I got all the dust bunnies.

"Nice place," he says.

"It's not much, but it's home," I say.

Luis looks at the awards and trophies on my shelf. I wonder if he thinks they're childish.

"You must think I'm being really stupid about this whole Andre thing," I say.

"I don't think you're stupid," Luis says. "Crushes make people do weird things."

"I wish I was as sure of myself as you are," I say. "If I was, I wouldn't need to go through all the effort of a promposal."

"I would be flattered if someone went through all this trouble to ask me to a prom," Luis says.

"You would?"

"Of course I would."

"I'm glad to hear that. After the story you told me about being ghosted by that dude, I was worried you had given up on love. You're a special guy, Luis. Even my dad said so."

"He did?"

"Just now. He thinks I should be asking you to the prom instead of Andre."

There's an awkward pause. I don't know what to say next. I was trying to pay Luis a compliment. But now I'm worried I've complicated things.

I'm relieved when Luis breaks the silence. "Do you ever read the 'Missed Connections' section of the *Georgia Straight*?"

"No. What is it?"

"It's for people who make eye contact with someone on the street or at a store. It lets them say what they wanted to say when they had the chance, but didn't. Can I show you on the computer?"

I open my laptop. Luis takes me to the page. We scroll through the list of people wanting to meet the person they saw locking up their bike, or walking to work, or standing behind them in line.

"You read this?" I ask.

"All the time." He smiles. "It's beautiful, isn't it? All of these people hopelessly in love with someone they've only seen for a few seconds. It makes me feel a little better about the world, knowing that love is all around us."

I watch Luis's face lit up by the computer screen. I'm starting to see him in a whole new light.

12 Missed Connection

As always, Geeda, Luis, and I are the first to arrive for the next meeting of prom advisory group.

"Why do we always have to be early, Charlie?" Geeda complains. "Just once I would like to get here after everyone else."

"Then we wouldn't get a good seat on the couch," says Luis. He carves out a space for himself in the corner. There's a devilish smile on his face.

"I'm glad you're here," Dave says to us. "I'm

dying for a cup of coffee. Do you three mind holding down the fort while I run to Melriches?"

"Go for it," I say.

Dave nearly runs face-first into Lottie as they rush into the Wreck Room. Lottie has figured out that if they want to sit next to Geeda on the couch, then they need to get here early, too.

"Is this seat taken?" Lottie asks. Lottie points to the space next to Geeda.

"It's all yours," Geeda says, batting her eyes.

I have to admit that I'm impressed by how Lottie is putting the moves on Geeda. I should start taking dating advice from them instead of some computer program.

Chad and Andre enter the Wreck Room five minutes later.

"Where's Dave?" Chad asks.

"Getting a coffee from Melriches," Geeda says.

"Hey, Andre," Luis says. He pulls his tablet out of his backpack. "Did you see this post in the 'Missed Connections' section of the *Georgia Straight*?"

Andre spins his head around like he's hearing

voices. Luis holds up his tablet to show Andre. It's like Andre is seeing Luis for the very first time. I wonder if the rest of us disappear from Andre's life as soon as we leave the room. Does he even remember my name?

"What is this *Georgia Straight*?" Andre asks, a little annoyed.

"A newspaper," I explain. "It covers local arts and left-leaning politics."

"And they have this whole section in the classifieds," Luis says. "You know, when you saw someone in public but didn't have the nerve to say something."

"The wit of the staircase," Andre says.

"Huh?" says Chad.

"The wit of the staircase," Andre says. "It's when you wish you introduced yourself to someone when you had the chance."

"The wit of the staircase is when you think of something to say after it's too late," Luis corrects him.

"It's a French expression," Andre sneers. "I think I know what the wit of the staircase is."

Actually, Luis is right. My English teacher uses the

expression all the time. I should defend Luis — he is my wingman after all. But I don't.

"People still write personal ads?" Chad says. "Isn't that what Tinder and Grindr are for?"

"This is more romantic," I say. "They're like love letters to perfect strangers."

"Look at this one," Luis says. He holds his tablet for Andre to see. "Doesn't this sound like you?"

Andre takes the tablet from Luis and holds it in front of his face.

"JIM DEVA PLAZA," Andre reads from the tablet. "You danced your way into my heart when you showed the plaza how to do The Floss. I thought the creepy guy with the man bun was your boyfriend. But I couldn't tell. Care to dance?"

"Let me see that," Chad says. He takes the tablet away from Andre.

"This is so cool, Andre," Lottie says. "No one does crap like this anymore. Are you going to answer his message?"

"I don't know," Andre says. "I'm flattered. But it's

sort of creepy. Why didn't he just say something in person instead of being all stalky about it?"

"Maybe he's shy," I say.

"Maybe he's homeless," Chad says.

"Aren't homeless people deserving of love?" Lottie says.

"I didn't mean it like that," Chad says, backtracking. "Maybe he's embarrassed that he doesn't have a home."

"Chad is right," Andre says. "I don't have anything against homeless people. But I don't want to date one."

What a horrible thing to say. I should delete the ad as soon as I get home. But then I look into the dark pools of Andre's brown eyes. It's like I can see right into his soul. He couldn't have meant what he said. He must have just said it wrong.

"What are you kids talking about?" Dave says. He's back with his cup of coffee.

"Someone left Andre a message in the 'Missed Connections' section of the *Georgia Straight*," Geeda tells him.

"People still do that?" Dave says. "I thought that's what Grindr was for."

Now that we're all here, we start the meeting. Today's meeting is to pick a DJ for the prom. We have four to choose from. Dave writes their names on the whiteboard. Then he plays a sample of their music, one by one. The first two sound almost the same — just sirens and bass. Andre and Chad both give those ones the thumbs up. The next one is a little bit better, but not much. The fourth DJ has us all bobbing our heads and singing along to classic Katy Perry and Taylor Swift. It's the winner, hands down.

"Congratulations, Chad, Charlie," Dave says. "You managed to get through that meeting without any drama."

Only because I have the upper hand, at last.

We're about to go our separate ways. Andre hasn't said anything about the 'Missed Connection' ad since before the meeting.

"Andre, you never said if you were going to

respond to that ad," Geeda says. Luis and I haven't told her about the promposal. But I'm sure she suspects Luis and I are the ones behind it.

"Of course he isn't," Chad says for him.

The temperature in the room rises as Andre's temper goes up. The glare in his eyes says that no one tells him what to do. Andre composes himself, like a model about to go out on the catwalk.

"Would you mind sending me the link on Facebook, um, Luis?" Andre asks. He pulls out his phone and taps it furiously. "You should get my friend request any second now."

Andre sashays out of the room, his chin in the air. He leaves Chad in his cologne-scented dust.

On the ride home, Luis and I are bursting at the seams trying not to say anything about what just happened. But it's all Geeda wants to talk about.

"Seems like everyone is trying to get a piece of Andre, huh?" Geeda says. "Charlie, I'm surprised you weren't as jealous as Chad was."

"I'm over Andre," I say. "It's clear he wants to be

with Chad. There's no point in tearing myself up over him."

"You're over him, just like that?" she says. "You move on really quick."

"I think I was able to convince Charlie he could do better," Luis says.

Geeda looks at both of us. She knows something is up. But we're at her house now. "Fine. Have it your way," she says as she gets out of the car.

I drive casually until we round the next corner. Then I pull over as soon as I can. Luis and I both starting bouncing up and down. We're squealing with joy at the success of our plan.

"I've never felt so powerful in all of my life," Luis says.

My phone chimes. I have a new email. I check my inbox. It's a message from the reply email in the *Georgia Straight*. It's from Andre. I show it to Luis and we both start screaming again.

This is the best day of my life!

13 Laying the Trap

I spend all the next week in touch with Andre by email. But Andre doesn't know it. He thinks he's emailing a stranger. I run every message past Luis before sending to Andre. I need to make sure I am striking the right balance between mystery and flirtation.

Maybe it's his Latin heritage, but Luis has a way with romantic emails. By the time he's done editing my messages, I start to fall for this made-up person myself. After the third email I begin to wonder if Luis is using them as a way to expose a part of himself. Maybe he wants me to see him as someone who deserves to be sought after. The way I'm seeking after Andre.

Andre is head over heels in love with his secret admirer. But he keeps pressing to meet in real life. I want to wait until we've finished watching season ten of *Drag Race*. What if Andre laughs in my face when he finds out that I'm his missed connection? I could never face him again. I would have to miss the final episodes.

At the next outNproud, Andre shows us the emails Luis and I have been sending him. More and more people have been showing up the closer we get to the end of season ten. There's little or no privacy for the six of us. I have to be careful not to mouth along with the latest email as Geeda reads it to us.

"The image of your face wipes away all my problems," Geeda reads from Andre's phone. "I can still see you dancing in my mind. It sets me free, like a bird gliding on the wind."

"He's laying it on kind of thick," says Chad. "I mean, he's only seen you once."

"Who's to say he's not in the room with us at this very moment?" Lottie says.

"Do you think so?" Andre says. His eyes snap to attention.

"It makes sense, doesn't it?" Lottie says. "We only socialize with maybe a third of the people who come here. Most of them aren't here every week."

"So, are you going to meet this guy or what?" Luis asks Andre.

"I want to," Andre says. "But he keeps putting it off. He won't even send me a picture of himself."

"That's a red flag if there ever was one," says Chad.

"Chad is right," Andre says. "This is the twenty-first century. Even my grandmother knows how to send a selfie."

"I still think you're being catfished," Chad says.

Chad is right, in a way. I might be the person sending the emails. But it's Luis's words Andre is falling for.

"I think it's romantic," Geeda says.

"What do you think I should do, Charlie?" Andre asks.

So he does know my name.

"I don't see the harm in meeting the guy," I say. "If he's not who you think he is, you can just go your separate ways. But be gentle."

I wait until after we have dropped Geeda at home. Then I say to Luis, "I guess it's time for the next phase of the plan. I have to ask him to the prom."

"Do you have any ideas of how you're going to ask him?" Luis asks.

"I was going to send him some flowers at school with a note attached."

"You have to do it in person," Luis says, staring out the window. "Otherwise you lose the element of surprise. And he needs to see your face or it will be too easy for him to say no."

"What do you suggest?"

"You've been wanting for me to tell you what to do the whole time, haven't you?" Luis sounds annoyed.

"No. I was honestly going to send him some flowers."

"Canadian boys don't know anything about romance," Luis huffs. "I knew it would come to this. So I already came up with a plan. Pull over."

I pull the car over to the side of the road. Luis opens his backpack and pulls out his tablet. He shows me a map dotted with little red pins.

"What are those?" I ask.

"Tiny free libraries."

"Like those wooden boxes where you can leave a book and take one for free?"

"Yes. You're going to leave clues for Andre in the ones I've marked on this map. He'll follow the clues to the next library until he ends up here, in the Pitch N Putt in Stanley Park. That's where you will ask him to the prom."

"I love it! What gave you the idea?"

"I play a lot of role-playing games. I like a good quest."

"But what if someone finds the clues before Andre does?"

"I thought of that already. You will put the clues in a copy of *The Da Vinci Code*. Every library has one. And no one ever takes *The Da Vinci Code*."

"This is such a good idea. I could kiss you right now."

That's when I realize that I *could* kiss Luis right now. I've been having the time of my life trying to get Andre to go out with me. And it's all because of Luis. I'm not even sure I care about going to the prom with Andre anymore. I just want to keep this feeling of doing something with another person. I look into Luis's face for some kind of signal that it's okay to kiss him.

"Save your kisses for Andre," Luis says.

And just like that, the feeling is gone. "You're right." And I was worried Luis would think I had a crush on him when I asked him over to watch movies.

"Do you want me to write the clues for you?" he asks. "I don't mind."

"That would be great. I'll write the email letting

him know when and where he can find the first clue."

"I should probably proofread that for you."

"You're not leaving me a lot to do."

"You'll have enough to do to make yourself handsome for the big reveal. Don't worry. I'll take care of everything."

I'll take care of everything is the most romantic thing anyone has ever said to me. It's usually me doing all the work.

I drop off Luis at home. Driving back to my place, I wonder if I'm making some horrible mistake. Should I stop playing this game with Andre and just ask Luis to go to the prom with me? It would make more sense.

I write the email to Andre explaining how to find me. It is the most romantic thing I have ever written. But it's not Andre I'm thinking about as I write it. It's Luis.

14 *Only the Lonely*

Luis and I get up at the crack of dawn. We hide clues inside the little lending libraries around the West End of Vancouver. Luis was right. Every one of them has a copy of *The Da Vinci Code*.

I grab a copy of *Fifty Shades of Grey* from the last little library. "I'm taking this," I say. "I want to know what all the fuss is about."

"It's mommy porn," Luis says.

"How would you know?"

"I read my mother's copy."

"Your mom has these books?"

"She's Catholic, she's not dead."

"I'll never look at your mom the same way again."

We go for a coffee at Delaney's on Denman Street. Most of the customers are single gay men in their forties and fifties. They are either reading the paper or swiping left or right on their phones. I don't know if I envy them or feel sorry for them. There's something appealing about being single at that age. But it has to be lonely.

"Do you think you'll ever get married?" I ask Luis.

"Are you proposing?"

"No, I'm prom-posing." I pause. "I'm serious. Do you see yourself getting married?"

Luis thinks about it. "I don't know. I like the idea of growing old with someone. I don't know if that's in my future. Do you think you'll get married?"

"I do. I have to admit it kind of hurt when Geeda said she didn't think I cared about relationships. It made me feel like this stone-cold jerk, you know?"

"I don't think she meant it as an insult. You've always struck me as someone with more important things on your mind than boys."

"I think about boys all the time."

"I see that now." Luis laughs. "Can I ask you something personal?"

"Why not?"

"How did it feel after your mother left you and your dad?"

"You're the first person who's ever asked me that."

"I can't imagine what it would be like to lose a parent that way. For all our secrets, I still feel close to my parents."

"I don't know how I feel about my mom anymore. Some days I'm really angry at her. Some days I really want to talk to her about my feelings. Like right now, with this whole Andre mess. I think she would have better advice than my dad. But then I remember she left us without even saying goodbye."

"Did she at least tell you why?"

"She met someone else at the restaurant where

she worked. He was a cook and he got a job at one of the camps up in the oil sands. When he left, she went with him."

"One more reason to switch to renewable energy."

"I never thought about it until now. But I didn't become active in queer politics until after she left. I'm starting to realize that was my way of coping. If I could save the world, I wouldn't have to deal with my feelings about her."

"So what changed?"

"Andre. He was the first person who ever paid attention to me as someone more than an activist. He was the first person to make me feel attractive."

Luis grows quiet for a second. I get the feeling there is something he is not telling me. I'm tempted to ask him what he is thinking. But I'm not sure it's the right time.

"We should get going," I say instead. "Andre will probably start looking for the clues soon."

There's a part of me that wants to take back all the clues and spend the rest of the day with Luis. I wonder if he feels the same way. But it's too late for that. We're in too deep. It wouldn't be fair to Andre not to show up after the last clue. It would only confirm everything Chad said about the whole "Missed Connections" ad.

We wait in my car near Nelson Park. The first clue is in a little library on a secret path on Mole Hill that connects Pendrell to Comox Street. We wait for about half an hour before we see Andre crossing the park.

"Oh my God," I say. "Chad is with him."

"Of course he is," Luis says. "Andre is probably trying to make him jealous."

"I can't wait to see Chad's face when he learns it was me who posted the ad."

Luis looks annoyed when I say this. "Sometimes I wonder if you like showing up Chad more than you like Andre."

"Of course I like Andre." But I'm half-wondering if Luis is right.

I start the car and inch up the street so we can keep an eye on them. Luis and I duck our heads below the window so they can't see our faces. We watch as they read the clue. Then they walk in the direction of the next library on the map.

The next clue is on Pacific Street near one of the old row houses. Andre and Chad seem to be enjoying the day as they come down the hill and look for the library. They look happy together. Again I doubt if this is the right thing to do. But not for my sake. For theirs. Maybe I should just leave them be.

We watch as they open the little cabinet and unfold the clue. Next they walk toward Stanley Park.

It takes them twenty minutes to get to the last clue, near the Pitch and Putt. I get out of the car and wait for them to arrive. Now I'll find out if this whole thing has been a complete waste of time. A part of me is worried Chad and Andre will laugh in my face when they see me. But there's no turning back.

I watch them as they enter the park and walk toward the little library.

I hear someone inside the Pitch and Putt yell, "Heads up!"

A golf ball arcs across the blue sky. I follow it with

my eyes. My jaw falls open as I watch it fall back toward the Earth. It's falling fast in Chad and Andre's direction. Neither of them is paying attention.

CLUNK!

The golf ball hits Andre squarely in the forehead. He falls onto grass.

"Someone help!" Chad shouts.

My first impulse is to run to see if Andre is okay. But I don't want to give myself away. A crowd forms around Andre. A minute later, sirens can be heard coming in our direction.

It's chaos. The medical personnel check to see if Andre is okay. I can see him sitting up a bit, holding his forehead. Then they get him on a stretcher and take him to the ambulance.

Chad scans the crowd. It's clear he's trying to figure out if Andre's secret admirer is lurking around. I duck behind my car so he can't see me. Then he gets into the ambulance with Andre and they drive off.

"We should go before someone sees us," Luis says.

I'm about to get back into the car when I

remember something. "I'll be right back," I say. I run to the little library and grab the envelope with the last clue inside. Back inside the car, I shove the envelope inside my bullet journal. Then we drive away.

15 *No Good Deed*

Andre isn't at the next prom advisory meeting. Before the meeting begins, Chad tells us all what happened in the park. Geeda and Lottie are shocked by the news at first. Then Geeda gets a case of the giggles.

"Is he all right?" she asks as she tries to control herself.

"There's swelling where the golf ball hit him. But the doctors don't think he has a concussion," Chad explains.

"Talk about your unforced errors," Lottie jokes.

"This isn't funny!" Chad says. "Andre could have been seriously hurt."

"Chad is right," Dave says. "This could have been way more serious."

Despite what Dave says, we can tell he thinks it's just a little bit funny. Even I'm amused at what happened, now that I know Andre is okay. But Chad is right. Andre could have been seriously injured. And it would have been my fault.

"Did you guys at least find out who posted the ad?" Lottie asks.

"The coward didn't show his face," says Chad bitterly. "I'm sure he saw the whole thing."

"What makes you so sure?" I ask.

"He would have had to have been there," he says. "You know, to meet Andre when he found the clue."

"How did you know it was the last clue?" I ask.

"I don't," Chad says. "How do *you* know it was the last clue?"

Uh oh.

Suddenly all eyes in the room are on me. How could I have been so stupid? I should have just kept my mouth shut. My palms become clammy. Sweat starts rolling down my forehead.

Luis comes to my rescue. "I think what Charlie was trying to say is that it would make sense that it was the last clue," he says. "Didn't you tell us you had already found two other clues?"

"What does that have to do with anything?" Chad asks.

"How many clues did you expect?" Geeda says. "It was a missed connection, not an Easter egg hunt."

"How do you even know it was a guy who was leaving the clues?" I blurt out. I'm trying to throw Chad off my trail. "For all we know it could have been a woman."

"I find that hard to believe," Lottie says.

"Me, too," says Dave. "I would be willing to believe that whoever was behind this is trans. Maybe they felt insecure about hitting on a cisgender male."

"Is it my imagination, or is Charlie acting funny?"

Chad asks the group. "Look at his shirt. He looks like he's run a mile. But he's barely moved."

"What the heck?!" I try to sound offended. "I'm as concerned for Andre as the rest of you are. I happen to sweat when I'm upset."

"You didn't seem very surprised to learn what happened when I told the group," Chad says.

"What did you expect? Tears?" I ask.

"Plus," adds Chad, "I always see you staring at Andre when I'm talking to him."

"Charlie, you have been acting really weird around Andre," Lottie observes. "I didn't want to say anything. But you've been way more aggressive toward Chad since Andre joined the group."

"I don't know what you're talking about," I say. "Ask Luis. Have I ever mentioned Andre to you?"

Luis starts to squirm in his seat. I can't tell if he's going to cover for me or spill the beans.

"Charlie did tell me he thought Andre was cute," Geeda says. "But think about it. It's Charlie. He's not romantic enough to go to the trouble of putting an ad in the paper. I mean, look at him. He only started caring about how he looked a couple of weeks ago."

I get that Geeda is trying to protect me. But she could be a little nicer about it.

"My point exactly!" Chad says, like a lawyer in a courtroom. "Remember how he dressed before? It was like he didn't even bother to look in the mirror before he left the house."

"Okay, everyone, tone it down a little," Dave says. "Charlie's wardrobe was never that bad."

Great. Now even Dave thinks I dress like a loser.

"Between homework and all the committees I sit on, I barely have time to myself," I say. "But putting more effort into my look had nothing to do with Andre."

"I'm not convinced," Chad says. "I could have sworn I saw your car pass us when we were looking for one of the clues."

This is not good. How do I get out of this? Then I get an idea. "I wasn't going to tell you this," I say. "But if you all must know, Luis and I have been dating for the last while."

Luis's eyes widen. The rest of the group is as shocked by the news as he is.

"That's so cute! Why didn't you tell me before?" Geeda asks.

"Well, you know how it is," I say. "We wanted to wait until we were sure."

Chad crosses his arms and stares daggers at me. "Well, isn't this convenient?" he says. He turns to Luis. "Luis, are the two of you really dating?"

This time, all eyes are on Luis. He squirms in his chair. Then he stands up. He takes my hand and gives me a kiss on the cheek.

"Yes, it's true," he says.

Geeda, Lottie, and Dave clap, the way people do when you announce that you're in a relationship. I used to think it was a lot of crap. But to be honest, it feels kind of good.

"Now that we've put this to rest," Dave says, "can we get on with the meeting?"

"Gladly," I say.

Luis squeezes my hand really hard before he lets go of it. I can tell from the energy coming off his body that he's not at all happy about my little announcement. This is confirmed after we leave the meeting and have dropped Geeda off at home.

"Are you crazy?" Luis asks me. "What were you thinking? Telling a lie like that."

"I didn't know what else to say. I was worried that if Chad kept pressing me I was going to crack."

"Then you should have cracked! What's the worst that could have happened?"

"Do you really need to ask that question? Chad would never let me forget it."

"So you decided it would be easier to drag me into your drama?"

"You were at the park, too! You're almost as much to blame for what happened as I am."

"Because I was helping you!"

"Then I guess we both made some poor life choices. What is the harm in pretending we're boyfriends? It's not like we don't hang out already. We can pretend to break up as soon as the prom is over."

"And what if I want to take someone else to the prom?" Luis asks.

"What are the odds of that happening?" I scoff.

I've never seen Luis look so angry. "You know what? I'll take the bus home," he says as he opens the car door.

"Don't be like that, Luis. I'm sorry. I didn't mean it that way."

"I need some time alone, Charlie. You just enjoy being you." He walks off into the evening.

16 Sorry

I haven't been able to sleep for two days. I keep tossing and turning in bed, trying to figure out how to make things right with Luis. I'm afraid that if I text or call him he'll just shut me down.

To make matters worse, Geeda has been all over me at school about my "relationship" with Luis. It was all she talked about today at lunch.

"I have to be honest," she says. "I totally thought you were the one behind that whole Andre thing. But as soon as you said that you and Luis were dating, it was like a light bulb went on in my head. Why didn't you say anything sooner? I thought you and I were friends!"

"I didn't want to jinx it," I say.

"I get it. Like waiting until you show before you tell people you're pregnant."

I smile and play along as if I'm not eating my heart out.

"Have you guys coordinated what you're going to wear to the prom?" Geeda asks.

I haven't even thought about my outfit for the prom until now. If this is what straight kids go through every year, they can have their stupid prom.

Dad is making dinner when I get home from school. The apartment is humid from the steam rising from a pot of boiling water. The air is filled with the smell of garlic. All of a sudden, I'm starving.

"I hope you don't mind pasta again," Dad calls out.

Instead of answering, I flop face-first onto the couch.

"Hey, sport. Are you okay?" Dad says, coming to check on me.

"I messed up my friendship with Luis."

"What's up?"

I tell dad the whole story. The "Missed Connections" ad, the promposal, the golf ball. And the lie I told at the drop-in. Dad shakes his head like he's just been spun around a million times.

"All that was going on under my nose, huh?" he says. "No wonder your mom found it so easy to cheat on me."

"I didn't think I was doing any harm," I say. "It was actually the most fun I've had in a long time."

"It's all fun and games until someone's heart gets broken."

"What am I going to do?"

"Tell Luis you're sorry."

"I did. But he won't listen."

"Then do it again. I hate to break it to you, but you're going to have to eat a lot of crow before this gets better."

"I wish I could go to sleep and wake up when all of this is over."

"Where's the lesson in that? If you ever want to be in a serious relationship, then you need to learn how to apologize."

"But Luis and I aren't dating."

"You could have fooled me," Dad says. "Come on. Get some carbs in you. You're going to need them for the drive to his place to tell him how you feel."

The carbs do make me feel better. But I still have no idea what to say to Luis. I practice a few things while I'm stuck in traffic. Nothing sounds right.

I hold my breath and press the entry code in the lobby.

His mother answers. "Who is it?" she asks.

"Charlie. Luis's friend. We met a few weeks ago."

"Oh." She sounds cautious, like I'm an intruder.

"Could I come up for a bit? I need to speak to Luis."

There's a pause. Then she says, "Okay."

I take the stairs instead of the elevator. I need to buy some time to think of what to say. Luis's mother opens the door. The TV is on, loud. At least Luis and I will be able to speak freely.

"Luis is in his room," his mother says. "He's been very sad lately."

"Me, too," I say.

"Did something happen with you two?"

"Sort of. It's complicated."

"Complicated . . ." Her voice trails off. I think I've just confirmed her worst fears about our relationship.

"There was a misunderstanding," I say. "I spoke without thinking."

"Men are good at that," she says.

Luis's mom steps aside to let me in. I follow her down the hall to his bedroom. She knocks on the door and says, "Luis, you have a visitor."

Luis looks confused when he opens the door and sees me. I can't tell if he's happy or angry that I'm here. His mom walks back to the living room, leaving us alone.

"Can I come in?" I say.

"So you can insult me again?"

"Please don't be like that. It was really hard for me to work up the nerve to come here."

"It's so hard being Charlie," he mocks.

"Sometimes it is. Like right now. If you're trying to make me feel worse, you can't. I'm as low as I can go."

"Good."

"Does that mean I can come in?"

Luis thinks about it and holds the door open.

"I really do love how clean your room is," I say, looking around.

"Is that supposed to make me feel better?"

"Of course not. But I hope this does. I want to tell you how sorry I am for what I said the other night. I didn't mean to imply you couldn't get a date for the prom. I just figured you're so closeted that you wouldn't risk it."

Luis mulls this over from his seat on the bed. He looks confused. And hurt. I feel horrible that I caused him so much pain.

"Sometimes I wonder if you hear yourself talk," Luis says. "You can be so rude sometimes."

"Like when?"

"Like every time you talk to Chad."

"That's different. It's not mean if it's true."

"But I never thought you would insult me like that. I thought you liked me."

"Are you kidding? You're the first male friend I've had in years! Sometimes I think the only reason I've continued with this little plan is so we can keep hanging out."

"It has been a lot of fun." Luis nods. "But then you reminded me that I didn't have a date for the prom. It was like reality clicked in. I realized I've been spending all this time helping you get a date and I haven't bothered finding one for myself."

"In that case," I say, "will you go to the prom with me?"

"Huh?"

"Will you go to the prom with me?" I repeat. Every time I say it, it feels more right.

"If you're asking me out of pity, then forget it."

"After all we've been through, who else could I possibly take?"

Luis thinks about it for just a moment. "Okay. I'll go with you. But if you think you're going to get lucky, then you have another thing coming. I'm still a Catholic."

"I promise to keep my hands above the waist the whole night." Dad was right. For two people who aren't dating, we sure act like it.

There's an awkward moment. I don't know if I should hug Luis or kiss him. We both kind of shrug our shoulders. And then we shake hands.

17 Sharp Dressed Man

I'm about to leave to pick up Luis. We're going shopping for our prom outfits. Dad stops me before I open the door.

"I wanted you to have this." He hands me an envelope. There are five twenties inside.

"Dad, I can't take this," I say. "The prom is just a glorified high school dance. I would rather you put this toward something we can share."

"This is something we can share," he says. "Your going to the prom is a big moment in both our lives.

I don't want you to look back on this time and wish you hadn't had to worry about money."

I look at the twenties. I don't know if I've ever held a hundred dollars in my hand at one time. My paycheque from London Drugs goes directly into my bank account. When I do spend money, I use my debit card.

"Don't forget to order a lapel flower for Luis," Dad says.

"What do I need to do that for?"

"It's tradition. The guy always gets a flower for his date."

"But we're both guys."

"So? Everyone loves to get flowers. Even guys. Don't trust anyone who doesn't."

I pick up Luis and we drive to Metrotown shopping centre. I'm not a huge fan of shopping malls. They make me feel like a cog in the wheel of society. But tonight, with Luis, all I want is to buy nice clothes.

"What do you see yourself wearing?" I ask Luis.

"I want to look nice," he says. "But I want to be able to dance."

As we walk through the mall I start to realize how happy I am. For the last few weeks all I've thought about is Andre. And about beating Chad to ask Andre to the prom. Now all that pressure is off me. I can be myself again. Whoever that is.

I notice that Luis is more relaxed, too. There's a spring in his step. He's not as quiet as he used to be. Our hands accidentally touch. I say, "I'm sorry," like I goosed him or something. I can't believe how weird I feel around him all of a sudden.

I know we're only pretending to be dating. But it does kind of feel like we're a couple. And you know what? I like it! Maybe if we have a good time at the prom, Luis and I can date for real.

Is that even possible? He can't possibly feel this way, too. Not after all we've been through. Still, I can't help but wonder what it would be like to kiss him. If for no other reason than to find out what it's like to kiss a boy.

"Are your parents okay with you going to the prom?" I ask as we browse at Old Navy.

"I told them I'm going to a Mexican dance,"

he says. "They think outNproud is a social group for Latino kids."

"Aren't they the least bit suspicious?" I ask. "They must know other Mexican families."

"None with kids my age."

"When I was over at your house the other day, I got the feeling your mom knew something. Like there's more to our friendship than being classmates."

"She hasn't said anything."

"Has it occurred to you that maybe your parents are waiting for you to tell them you're gay?"

"No," he says, leaving it at that.

I can see how my feelings for Luis are like his feelings for his parents. We both have this huge secret. But we're too afraid to share it with someone we care about out of fear of being rejected.

"I always get nervous around your mom," I say. "The whole Catholic thing."

"Don't be. She likes you. She was very impressed when you came to our house to apologize."

"You can thank my dad for that. It was his idea."

"Your father seems very nice. It's sad that he's alone."

"He has me."

"You know what I mean."

"You'll never believe what he said."

"What?"

"It's too embarrassing. Forget it."

"Tell me."

Should I lie? Or should I tell him my dad thinks Luis is the one I should be dating? If I do, this could get really awkward really fast. I was just starting to enjoy things the way they are. But I can't keep hiding my feelings.

"He said that I should be trying to date you instead of Andre."

Luis starts to blush. "He said that? Really?"

"He feels that anyone who would write a computer program for me is probably a good catch."

"That was nice of him to say."

"Yeah, it was."

Luis pulls a pair of black khakis off the rack. He holds them up for me to see. "What do you think of these?"

"For me or for you?"

"For you."

"They're nice. And they're on sale! Do you mind if I try them on?"

"Please do."

I take a moment in the dressing room. I need to figure out what is going on between Luis and me. Is he not getting the fact that I'm interested in him? Or is he as bad at this whole dating thing as I am? What do I have to do? Hire a plane to write "kiss me" in the sky?

I step out of the dressing room to show Luis how I look in the khakis. "What do you think?" I ask him.

"Turn around," he says. I do as I'm told. "They make your butt look really good."

Now I'm totally confused. Is he complimenting my butt because he likes what he sees? Or so that I will buy the stupid khakis? Screw it. I'm buying the stupid khakis.

Two hours later we've both managed to find what we were looking for. We stop at the food court and share an order of fries before we call it a night.

"I didn't know you like to dance," I say.

"I'm Mexican. Of course I like to dance."

"That's kind of a racist thing to say, isn't it?"

"Not when you're Mexican."

"I have a confession to make," I say.

Luis looks a little panicked. This is exactly why I don't want to tell him how I really feel.

"I have two left feet," I say.

Luis looks under the table. "Not according to your shoes," he says.

"You know what I mean."

"Dancing is easy. You just have to relax and follow the music."

"Easy for you to say. You're Mexican."

"That's racist."

"But you just said..." It's my turn to look panicked.

"I was only kidding," Luis laughs. "I like making you flustered."

If he only knew.

18 Caught

It's the last meeting before the prom. All that is left to do is go over the floor plan for the venue. Dave explains that everyone coming into the venue needs to have their bag searched and checked into the coat check.

Alarm bells start going off in my head. "You're searching our bags? And making us check them as well? That sounds pretty invasive," I say.

"It's for our security," Chad says. Figures he would defend a bag search.

"I doubt some queer teen from Squamish is going to sneak a gun into the queer prom," I say.

"This has nothing to do with security," Dave says. "This is a sober event. The sight of alcohol could trigger someone in recovery."

"High school dances are sober events," Geeda says. "People sneak booze into them all the time."

"Sadly, queer events are held to a higher standard," Dave says. "We're lucky we've never been picketed before. It's best if we don't attract the attention of the religious right."

"Aren't you supposed to be teaching us to be out and proud?" Luis asks. "It sounds like you're telling us to slip under the radar."

Dave looks up at the ceiling. We can tell he's trying to find a proper answer to Luis's question. It's obvious he's struggled with this before. I don't envy his role as our ethical advisor.

"I would never tell anyone in this room to pretend be something they are not," Dave says. "But the time will come when people who want take away your rights will show up on your doorstep. Until then, I think it's important we all have a good time."

Dave goes over some of the smaller details of the prom. He shows us the email he's going to send to the surrounding school districts. Then he asks us if we would all share the Facebook event on our timelines.

"I can't," Luis says. "I'm not out to my parents."

"That's fine, Luis," Dave says.

"How many people are we expecting?" Geeda asks Dave.

"Last year we had just under three hundred people," he says.

"Wow!" says Lottie. "That's a lot of work."

"It will be fine," Dave says. "We have a ton of volunteers to help out."

Then comes the fun part. Dave gives us samples of the snacks they want to serve. Then we each get to taste some of the mocktails that will be on sale. I ask the most questions. I want to make sure that every aspect of the prom appeals to the broadest number of people at the event. Chad rolls his eyes every time I open my mouth. But I don't care.

The meeting lasts a couple of hours. When we're done I close my bullet journal for the evening. When I go to put it in my backpack, a white envelope falls out of it. It flutters to the ground like a pair of wings. It stops at Chad's feet.

The output from Luis's computer program flashes through my mind. *All of your secrets will be exposed.*

Chad bends over to pick up the envelope. He's about to hand it back to me, but he takes another look at it.

"This looks familiar," he says.

"That's personal!" I say. "Can I have that back, please?" I can hear the panic growing in my voice.

"Oh my God!" Andre says. "It's one of the clues from my secret admirer!"

Chad opens the envelope. He pulls out the last clue from that fateful day. "You're right, Andre!" Chad says. "I knew Charlie was the one behind all that!"

"I thought you and Luis were dating," Geeda says. She sounds disappointed.

"It was a smokescreen, Geeda," Lottie says gently.

"Is this true?" Geeda asks.

Luis and I look at each other like we just got caught with our hands in the cookie jar.

"Yes. It's true," I say. "I wanted to ask Andre to the prom. But I didn't know how. Luis was kind enough to help me put together a promposal. It was working perfectly until that stupid golf ball hit Andre in the head."

"This sounds like a plot in a *Scooby Doo* cartoon," Lottie says. "All that needs to happen now is for Luis to pull off a mask and reveal he's really Charlie."

"So, Charlie, you and Luis aren't dating?" Geeda asks.

I want to tell her that we are. I look at Luis. I look for some sign that he feels the same way. Instead, Luis looks at his feet and shakes his head — no.

I should feel relieved that the truth is out in the open. But in the end all I feel is sad. I really thought Luis and I had made a connection while we were shopping for prom clothes. I guess it was all just in my head.

"That kind of bums me out," Geeda says. "I

thought you two made a really cute couple."

At least Andre is happy. "Charlie, I can't believe you went to all that trouble to ask me to the prom," he says. "This has to be one of the nicest things anyone has ever done for me."

"It was Luis's idea," I say. "He wrote all the clues."

"But you were the one who put himself out on the line," Andre says. "That's so brave."

"Have you lost your mind?" Chad explodes. "He lied to you! And then he sent you on a wild goose chase around the city. And to top it off, you got knocked in the head by a golf ball!"

"Isn't it romantic?" Andre says.

Chad throws up his arms like the world has gone completely insane. It has, in a way. This is not the reaction I was expecting from Andre.

Andre walks over to me and takes me by the hands. He looks into my eyes and says, "Charlie, will you go to the prom with me?"

I don't know what to say. If Andre had asked me a week ago I would have been over the moon. But now

I'm not so sure. True, Chad is green with envy. It would give me a lot of pleasure to see the look on Chad's face if I say yes.

And then I see Luis is looking at me, waiting for my answer. I've already hurt Luis once this week. I couldn't do something as mean as cancel our prom date. Besides, I already bought him a lapel flower.

"I already told Luis I would go with him," I say.

"Oh, you don't have to pretend to go with him anymore," Andre says. "I forgive you for sending me to the hospital in an ambulance. Destiny has brought us together. You don't mind, Luis, do you?"

Now it's Luis's turn to say what he really feels.

"It's all right," he says. "You two go and have a good time."

Andre hugs me tight. I can feel his body through his clothes and smell the lotion on his skin. I feel like I'm being embraced by a photo in a magazine. I hug him back. For a brief second, it's like we were meant to be together.

19 Wheels

Andre has not stopped texting me since he asked me to the prom. It was fun at first. But now he's beginning to annoy me.

For one thing, Andre communicates almost purely through emojis. I don't know what he's trying to say half the time. He'll send me a text with five smiling faces, a dancing lady, and a devil. It's like trying to read the paintings in an Egyptian tomb. Even Geeda doesn't know what they mean.

At first I replied by saying LOL. That worked for a while. At least, until he replied, "I was being serious." So I started replying with a series of random emojis of my own: praying hands, a rainbow, a palm tree, and fireworks. We've been carrying on a conversation like this for more than a day now. I still have no idea what we're talking about.

I finally call Andre. I ask him if he would like a ride to the *Drag Race Reunion* show at outNproud on Friday.

"You have a car?" Andre sounds surprised.

"My dad bought it for me when I turned sixteen."

"Why am I only learning about this now?"

Because you only started paying attention to me when you learned I was your secret admirer, I think.

I arrange to pick up Andre at his house in Kitsilano. Geeda whistles as we drive by some of the homes. They all look like they belong in one of the many American TV shows that are filmed here.

"His family must be loaded to live in this part of town," she says. "What do his parents do?"

"I don't know."

"What do you mean you don't know? Don't you guys talk?"

"Not really. My calls always go to voicemail. He usually texts back a few minutes later."

"Are you any closer to him than you were on Saturday?"

"I know he's really fond of the mirror ball emoji."

"What do you see in this guy?" Geeda asks.

"His big, shiny eyes. His silky smooth skin. His firm, round butt. How he always smells of coconut."

"Are you describing a person or your favourite ice cream? I think you need to break off your date with him to the prom. You need to ask Luis to go with you instead."

"I can't do that! Not after all the trouble I went through to get Andre to go with me."

"You can't justify going out with someone you don't like. Especially because of the time you invested in them, Charlie."

"I like Andre!" I say.

"Not the way you like Luis."

"Luis is my wingman. At least he was my wingman. I'm not even sure we're still friends."

"You and Luis are more than friends."

At least someone thinks so.

I'm thankful that I find Andre's address before we go any further down this rabbit hole. I honk the horn to let Andre know we're here. We wait ten minutes before he opens the door and bounces out of the house. His mood changes when he sees my car. It's like he's worried someone is going to see him near it.

"Something wrong?" Geeda asks.

"I was expecting a nicer car," Andre says.

"My BMW is in the shop," I say.

Andre lights up. "Really?"

"That's a joke, Andre," Geeda says through the window.

Andre pretends to laugh. No one has ever judged me for my car before. Most people my age are glad not to take the bus.

Andre waits outside the front passenger door.

"Aren't you going to get in?" Geeda asks.

Then she realizes Andre expects to ride shotgun. This is awkward. Geeda always rides shotgun. But she climbs into the back seat of the car without a fuss.

Andre gets into the car. He gives me a quick peck on the cheek. Stars circle my head. I'm not sure if I should be driving while feeling this light-headed.

"Now that I've seen your wheels," Andre says, "I'm glad that I went ahead and rented a limo for the prom."

"A limo?" I say. "That sounds expensive."

"It's only a hundred and fifty dollars," Andre says.

"Between the two of us?" I ask.

"Each."

A hundred and fifty dollars is half my paycheque. We could take a cab for a third of the price. But I can't say anything. Andre will think I'm cheap. Or worse, poor! Both of which are true.

They've already started watching *Drag Race* when we get to outNproud. I try not to be annoyed. I don't want to scare off Andre with my need to be early for everything.

Chad, Luis, and Lottie are saving spots for us on the couch in the Wreck Room. Chad is stone-faced when he sees Andre and me walk into the room arm in arm. This is amazing. Sometimes the underdog actually does win.

"Hi, Luis," I say.

It's the first time we've talked to or seen each other since Andre asked me to the prom. I feel like such a jerk for cancelling on Luis. But it's his fault as much as mine. He could have told Andre that he still wanted to go to the prom with me. Then again, I could have said something, too. I guess we were both afraid of what the other would think.

The reunion show is an explosive one. Two of the queens get into a huge fight. Then one of them, The Vixen, walks out of the show.

Andre makes a big deal of cuddling up next to me on the couch. He moves his face close to my neck and inhales.

"You smell so good," Andre whispers. "What is your cologne?"

"Dove shower gel," I say. This is a lie. I use a no-name brand because it's cheaper.

"I'll have to try that," Andre says. He looks at Chad from the corner of his eyes. I start to wonder if I'm not the only one enjoying getting a rise out of Chad.

Luis, Lottie, and Geeda are having their own conversation on the other end of the couch. Luis says something. Lottie lets out a laugh that reminds me of a goose honking.

"What are you guys talking about?" I ask.

"Luis was telling us something funny that happened at school," Lottie says.

"Tell me," I say. "I could use a good laugh."

"The show's back on!" Andre says, shushing me.

Luis, Lottie, and Geeda grimace over their crime of talking during *RuPaul's Drag Race*. Andre snuggles closer into my shoulder. I lean my head against his.

"Can you not do that?" Andre says. "It hurts my neck."

20 To-Do List

It's the day before the prom. School let out a week ago, so I have all of Friday and Saturday to prepare. I'm more nervous about the queer prom than I thought I was going to be. I used to dream about being seen in public with Andre. Now I feel like I'm out of my league.

I go through my bullet journal. I review the checklist of things I need to do before the prom.

Iron my clothes.

Buy a new razor.

Get money from the ATM.

Get my hair trimmed.

Pick up the lapel flower.

The lapel flower. How could I have forgotten the lapel flower? I showed the florist a picture of Luis and asked her to pick a flower that would go with his eyes. What am I going to do with it now? I can't give it to Andre. It would be like cheating on Luis.

My phone vibrates. A flurry of emojis fills my screen. I don't have time to decipher Andre's code, so I call him.

He picks up on the first ring. "I'm so glad you called," Andre says, breathless. "I'm freaking out!"

"What's the matter?"

"I don't know what to wear to the prom."

"Do you have an idea of how you want to look?"

"Fabulous."

"That narrows it down."

"I don't have time for your sarcasm," Andre pouts into the phone. "I want to turn heads when I make my entrance."

"Why? You already have a date."

Andre doesn't say anything. It feels like I've caught him cheating on me. I should call this off right now and save us both a lousy evening. Why is doing the right thing always so hard?

"Can you come over?" Andre asks.

"Now?"

"Of course now."

"The prom is in twenty-four hours. You have plenty of time to make up your mind. Plus, I have a long list of things I need to do before tomorrow. Don't you want me to look good, too?"

"If I look good, you look good," Andre says. There's a hint of meanness in his voice. Like I should consider myself lucky to be going to the prom with someone like him.

"I'll be there in twenty minutes," I sigh.

Andre's room is strewn with clothes. I never knew anyone could have so many clothes. Some of them still have the price tags on them. He has so many outfits to choose from. How can he not be able to decide what to wear?

"I was thinking of something dressy but comfortable," Andre says.

"How about these?" I hold up a black short-sleeved dress shirt and a pair of stretchy silver pants.

"That looks like I'm going for a job interview as a host at a restaurant." I'm almost afraid to show him something else. Luckily, I don't have to. Andre proceeds to give me a private fashion show of all his favourite clothes. He makes me sit on a chair at the other end of the hall from his bedroom. Outfit by outfit, Andre emerges from his room in a new ensemble. He parades by me like the queens doing the runway on *Drag Race*.

This is clearly not the first time Andre has used the hallway as a catwalk. He walks like a supermodel. He clomps down the carpet, never making eye contact with me. He sashays toward me, stops, turns, and clomps back to his room.

I start getting hungry after about thirty minutes. I'm barely paying attention to what he's wearing anymore. All his clothes start to blend into each other. The shirts highlight his chest and shoulders. His pants hug his butt. I just want it to be over so I can go home.

"Well? Which one did you like the best?" Andre asks.

"The third one?"

"Was that the jacket and black pants with a T-shirt? Or the kilt and the dress shirt?"

"Definitely the jacket, pants, and T-shirt," I say. I hate kilts on anyone but bagpipers. And even they work my nerves.

"That's so pedestrian," Andre says. "Anybody could pull that off."

"I'm wearing black pants, a white shirt, and a bow tie," I say.

"Oh." Andre doesn't bother to apologize.

Should I buy another outfit? I can't. I've already

spent the money Dad gave me. I need to dip into my savings to pay for the stupid limo.

"Let me try on one more outfit," Andre says.

"I have a shift at the store tonight," I lie. "I need to get going if I'm going to be on time."

"You didn't say anything before."

"I didn't know it would take this long."

Andre walks me to the door. He's still wearing the last outfit from his fashion show. I feel underdressed next to him. I turn to face him before I leave. I expect him to give me a peck on the cheek or at least a hug goodbye.

"The limo arrives at six p.m.," is all he says. "I should be at your place by six-thirty. That should get us to the prom at around seven, depending on the traffic."

"I'll be ready, I promise."

I'm home before Dad, so I decide to make a pot of chili and some garlic toast. I let the chili simmer and go back to my bullet journal. I see notes I made when Luis and I were putting the promposal together. They make me feel warm and fuzzy. I miss hanging with him.

I call Luis. I'm about to hang up when he answers the phone.

"Sorry it took me so long to pick up," Luis says. "I couldn't find my phone."

I can tell he's lying. He was probably staring at his phone, trying to decide whether or not to answer it. That's what I would do.

"Are you ready for the big night tomorrow?" I ask.

"I'm super excited! Especially now that I have a date."

"You have a date?" I feel jealous. "Who are you going with?"

"Chad."

I clamp my hand to my chest. Now I'm the one who feels like he's been hit in the head with a golf ball.

"When did this happen?" I ask.

"A couple of days ago. I was feeling sorry for myself because I didn't have anyone to go with. Then I remembered that Chad didn't have a date, either. I asked him over Facebook Messenger. He said yes almost right away."

"How could you go to the prom with my enemy?"

"Chad is only your enemy in your mind. Do you really think he spends his days trying to figure out how to get under your skin? This war you're having with him is all about you, not him."

"You know he only said yes to make Andre jealous."

"So? Andre is going to the prom with you for the same reason. And the only reason you're going with Andre is to piss off Chad."

"That's not true. I'm very fond of Andre."

"Name one thing you like about him."

"He speaks French."

"But you don't."

Luis is right. I don't. Andre could insult me to my face in French. I wouldn't have the slightest idea what he was saying.

"What do you like about Chad?" I ask.

"He didn't have a date for the prom," Luis says. And then he hangs up the phone.

21 The Prom

I'm getting ready to go to the prom. I shave twice after I take my shower. My hands are shaking. It's amazing I don't cut myself with the razor. I do some deep breathing as I get dressed. It doesn't help. I put the buttons in the wrong holes and have to undo and do up my shirt all over again. I try tying my tie following instructions on YouTube but it looks like the ribbon on a present.

"Dad? Can you help me with my tie?" I shout from my room.

"I thought you would never ask." Dad runs in to help. He spins me around so I'm facing him.

"How do I look?" I ask.

"Like Prince Charming," he says, looping the tie around itself. "Is Luis going to be there tonight?"

"Yes. He's taking my enemy, Chad."

"Burn! That will teach you for getting on his bad side. I can't say I blame him. That was a rotten thing you did to him."

"We've been through this already, Dad. Andre is my date. Any guy would be lucky to go to the prom with him."

"There's nothing wrong with rooting for the underdog." Dad spins me back around to face my dresser mirror. "You could get married in that outfit."

The apartment buzzer rings. Dad runs out of my room to let Andre into the building. I run into the kitchen and grab the lapel flower from the fridge. It's a single red rose with a little bit of Baby's Breath around it. Then I wait by the door for Andre to arrive. Now I'm excited about going to the prom again. Yesterday's fashion show is a distant memory.

I open the door for Andre. He's wearing the kilt and a silver see-through shirt. Why is he wearing the kilt? No one looks good in a kilt.

"You look like a waiter," Andre says.

Well, he looks like a reject from *So You Think You Can Dance*.

"I told you yesterday that this is what I would be wearing," I say.

"I must not have been paying attention."

"I got this for you." I hand him the rose.

"What am I supposed to do with that?"

"Pin it to your shirt," Dad says. He holds out his phone, ready to take pictures.

"I don't want to put holes in my shirt," Andre says. "It was expensive."

"I'll pin it to my lapel, then. You can take it home with you," I say, doing my best to keep the peace.

Dad does not look amused.

"We should get going," Andre says.

"Can't we take some pictures first?" Dad asks.

"We don't have time," says Andre. "The limo is waiting."

"It will only take a minute," Dad says.

Andre doesn't want to take a picture with me. It says a lot about our date. Andre never had me in mind when he planned on going to the prom. The limo, his outfit . . . they were all meant for Chad, not for me. I'm glad Andre doesn't want to take pictures. The sooner this night is over, the sooner I can put it behind me.

"I'll send you some pictures from the prom," I say to Dad. "I promise."

"Okay," Dad says. I give Dad a hug and follow Andre out the door.

We get inside the waiting limo. It's just a Town Car. I don't know why it's costing so much. We get stuck in traffic as soon as we get downtown. Andre and I barely say a word to each other. He keeps pulling the kilt over his knees like it's a skirt.

There's a crowd of people waiting to get into the Roundhouse Community Centre. I get a lump in my throat seeing such a diverse group of queer people my age, all in one place. It's like I'm looking at the queer community of the future and it gives me a lot of hope.

Andre grabs my hand and leads me through the crowd. He's almost pushing people out of his way. I'm not comfortable with it. We finally find Geeda, Lottie, Chad, and Luis near the entrance.

My heart skips a beat when I see Luis. He's wearing a white shirt and black pants like me. He has a bow tie, too. We look like a pair of plastic grooms you stick on top of a wedding cake.

"Hey, Andre." Chad is being casual. "Hey, Charlie."

Charlie. If I had known stealing Andre from Chad would get him to say my name right, I would have done it weeks ago.

"Hey, Chad," I say. "Hey, Luis."

"Is this a rumble?" Geeda asks.

That's when I notice that Geeda and Lottie are at the prom together.

"When did this happen?" I ask Geeda, gesturing between the two of them.

"It's been happening for weeks," she says.

"Slow and steady wins the race," Lottie says. They have a big grin on their face.

The music starts up inside. The crowd cheers and begins to fidget in place. Everyone is ready to get the party started. The doors open and we slowly begin to shuffle inside.

I'm amazed at how great the place looks. A giant mirror ball revolves above the dance floor. It sprinkles light around the room like pixie dust. The room is hung with metallic fabric and streamers. The dance floor looks like a sea of stars.

Geeda and Lottie run onto the dance floor and spin each other around. They already look like they're having the time of their lives.

"What do you think of the decorations?" says someone from behind me. It's Dave. He's wearing a tuxedo shirt that's been cut off at the sleeves and black suspenders.

"They're amazing," I say. "I was worried they were going to look tacky."

"They are tacky," Dave says. "It's just a trick of the light."

"Thanks for putting up with me on the committee," I say. "I know I can be a little bossy. I've been trying to mellow out."

"Don't mellow out too much," he says. "The community needs people like you to get things done."

"Can you tell my dad that?"

"The six of you should be really proud of yourselves," Dave says. "We couldn't have put this together without you."

"I feel like all we did was argue."

"You did more than argue, you participated. You gave up your Saturdays to make sure the adults didn't impose what they wanted on your prom. Not a lot of people would do that."

I get a small lump in my throat. Most people think I participate because I'm in it for myself. But I really do want to make things better for everyone.

"Now go out there and find your date," Dave says. "You have some dancing to do."

Andre has disappeared on me. I circle the dance floor to look for him. I find him on the opposite side of the room from where Luis and Chad are standing. I look across and watch Luis try to talk to Chad. Chad is only half-listening. He's too busy staring at Andre.

"Let's dance," Andre says. He pulls me onto the dance floor.

"Make Me Feel" by Janelle Monae is playing. I have no idea how to dance to this song. I try to move my hips to the beat of the music. But it feels like I'm tripping over my feet.

Andre starts using me as a stripper pole. He grinds his crotch against mine. Then he turns around and does the same thing with his butt. I should be getting turned on. But all I feel is embarrassed.

The next thing I know, Luis and Chad are dancing next to us. Chad starts twerking. He shakes his ass in Luis's direction. Luis looks confused and uncomfortable. He smiles half-heartedly and dances on his own.

Now Andre starts twerking. He's way better at it than Chad is. I find myself backing away from Andre. Chad takes my place. Soon he and Andre are twerking at each other, trying to outdo one another. Their butts bob up and down. A circle forms around them until I'm pushed aside. I can't see them through the crowd.

22 Truth on the Dance Floor

I walk off the dance floor. I keep walking until I get to the reception area. People are still lining up to get into the prom. They look happy and excited. I can only imagine what I look like to them.

"Hey, Charlie!" Geeda shouts to me. She and Lottie have their arms around each other. They're glistening with sweat. "Why aren't you on the dance floor with Andre?"

"I've been replaced," I tell her.

"I hate to say I told you so," Geeda says. "But I told you so."

"I'll be sure to write that in my bullet journal when I get home tonight."

"Come hang out with us," Lottie says. "Don't let that jerk ruin your good time. This is your prom as much as his."

"I think I'll just go home," I say.

"I won't let you." Geeda pulls my arm. "I insist you have a good time."

Lottie grabs my other arm and the two of them drag me back to the dance floor. I resist at first, but they're too strong. They lead me out beneath the mirror ball. We start to dance in a circle to a Lady Gaga song. I actually love the song, but my heart isn't in it.

"I'm going to get something to drink," I say when the song is over.

"Promise me you're not going to leave," Geeda says.

"I promise."

I start to make my way through the crowd to the

bar to get myself a mocktail. Then my worst nightmare comes to life. From the edge of the dance floor I see Andre making out with Chad. They're slow dancing, even though the song is upbeat. It's like they're dancing to the beat of their own hearts.

How could I have been so stupid as to let Andre lead me on? Everyone and their dog warned me Andre was using me to get to Chad. Why didn't I believe them? Instead I ruined the prom for myself and ruined my friendship with Luis.

I turn back toward the reception area. I can't be here anymore. I'll text Geeda on the way home and let her know what happened.

There are almost as many people in the reception area as on the dance floor. I'm stuck. Someone taps me on the shoulder. I turn around, expecting to see Geeda. But it's Luis.

"Happy now?" he says. His arms are crossed over his chest.

"I should be asking you the same thing," I say. "None of this would have happened if you had just told Andre it wasn't okay for him to take me to the prom!"

"What did you expect me say? I had just spent the last two weeks trying to help you get Andre to go to the prom with you. I didn't want you spending the night wishing you were at the dance with him instead of me."

"I thought I made it obvious I liked you as more than a friend."

"You didn't. And you know what I went through before. I wasn't going to put my heart on the line again."

"I didn't know how to tell you how I felt," I say. "Every time I dropped a hint, it was like you couldn't change the subject fast enough."

"I wanted to believe that you liked me as more than a friend, Charlie. But I needed to be sure. I didn't want to make a fool of myself again."

"I'm telling you now," I say. "These last few weeks we've hung out together have been some of the best times of my life. I know I didn't tell you I had feelings for you. It was only because I didn't know what it was like to have a crush on someone for who they are instead of how they look."

"Is this the passionate speech the computer program was talking about?"

"I think so."

We stand there like a pair of idiots, looking at each other. I decide to take a chance. I wrap my arms around Luis. The lapel flower gets crushed between our bodies.

"Oh my God!" I say. "I got this for you!"

I take the rose off my lapel and pin it on his shirt. If he cares that I'm poking a hole in his shirt, he doesn't say anything. The flower really does bring out his eyes.

Suddenly the prom song, "I Melt With You," starts to play. The crowd cheers its approval.

"Let's dance," Luis says.

"Wait! Can we take a picture for my dad?"

"Of course!"

I hold my phone above our heads. We smile as we wait for the flash to go off.

I move awkwardly, trying to keep up with the beat

of the music. I feel like an idiot and stop in place.

Luis puts his hands on my shoulders and says, "Relax. Just follow the beat. Just follow me."

He takes my hands and swings them back and forth. Soon we're bouncing around on the dance floor like kids in a bouncy castle. Geeda taps me on the shoulder as she and Lottie join us. The four of us start dancing in a circle.

The song ends. Luis and I wrap our arms around each other and kiss for the first time. I'm not sure if we're spinning or if it's the motion of the mirror ball. But it feels like flying. My phone vibrates in my pocket. It's a text from my dad: a thumbs-up emoji.

Acknowledgements

As always, I would like to thank Kat Mototsune for her guidance and advice throughout the development of this book. I can't stop seeing your space kitty backpack everywhere I go now. Thank you to Lisa Wong for introducing me to the weird and wonderful world of bullet journals. I'm in awe of your organizational skills. And thank you to the staff at Qmunity in Vancouver for explaining how queer youth drop-ins and queer proms work. Queer youth are lucky to have an organization like yours on their side.